For Susan,
a fellow lover
of the woo.
Stay magical*⚡*

WOUNDED

GRETA T. BATES

This is a work of fiction. Names, characters, places, and incidents are products of the author's imagination or are used fictitiously and are not to be construed as real. Any resemblance to actual events, locations, organizations, or persons, living or dead, is entirely coincidental.

World Castle Publishing, LLC
Pensacola, Florida
Copyright © 2023 Greta T. Bates
Hardback ISBN: 9798891260450
Paperback ISBN: 9798891260467
eBook ISBN: 9798891260474
First Edition World Castle Publishing, LLC, September 12, 2023
http://www.worldcastlepublishing.com

Cover: Adam Martin
Editor: Karen Fuller

Please Note:
Please note that *Wounded* contains scenes with self-harm and mental issues and may not be suitable for all readers. Reader discretion is advised.

"And she saw the world not always as it was, but as perhaps it could be with just a little bit of magic."

-*Cinderella* 2015

CHAPTER 1

NOW

"For many moons, I've toiled. The process has proven futile. I clean, I scour, I go into the cracks and crevices, and it is never enough. I've been made a maid in my own temple, my own home. Even in the shadows where I've flashed a light to find the grime, I've dusted and swept remnants into a receptacle only to realize time and again there is more work to do. So I stay, sullen, wallowing in the cinders, eyes swollen from so many shed tears in tattered clothes, typically dirty faced, smeared and smudged with ash.

"Days, years passing, spending time, fluctuating from bouts of melancholy and lightning quick surges of mania. There were days of productivity, trying and trying again, hoping to be seen, to be enough. Hungry *for attention. But there were many more days of barely doing what needed to be done then, outing the lights, drawing the curtains, and the descent into darkness would..."*

I tossed the pages onto the floor. What a pile of shit! This was not how I was supposed to be spending the summer before my senior year, going through my mom's things: piles of paper, boxes, drawers, scraps of scribblings. My mom, now locked away for safe keeping, thought she was a writer. She was always looking for that 'big break' in one way or another. But her words, her personality, it was all so overly emotional, so self-involved. Me, me, me. Just all her. She was constantly reliving her pain and trying to make anyone she came in contact with do the same. There was never a short answer to, "How was your day?" It was always something like, "Well, you think you have it bad? Let me tell you what happened to me." And then you got the Debbie Downer story, and it didn't even have to be about her. Sometimes, it was about somebody in town, and more often than not, you got some sad story she'd seen on TV. Anything to bring the conversation back to herself, her taking on somebody else's pain to get into the spotlight.

"Can't you see how miserable I am?" That was the gist of every conversation I ever had with her, if you could call it a conversation. It was usually one-sided. Classic narcissism. Her moods — up and down and up and down — withdrawing, attacking. Until it was time for the padded cell.

I can't speak for my grandmother, but my mom, she was part of that generation, the women who wanted to be rescued, the 'someday my prince will come' damsels in distress. Those women they all had the Princess Obsession. I blame all those fucking Disney movies. The princess wants to be rescued, the shoe fits perfectly, she and the prince live happily ever after. Anthropomorphic creatures dancing and singing, 'The End' appears in cursive, fireworks go off, and as the screen fades to dark, we're left with the happy couple kissing. Puke. Were they kissing? Or was she waving goodbye? Here I was, only 17, and I knew the world definitely didn't work that way. I'd seen the movies, too, but my logical brain knew that was a different time. When we'd left Mom at The Spa, I glimpsed her as I looked back through that tiny, glazed window on the door, all smiles, waving like the gal at the end of the movie. No glass slipper, though. No shoes at all. Was she finally having her happily ever after, too far gone to realize she was never getting out of this particular hole?

I'd spent my life tiptoeing around her, trying not to set her off, trying not to send her into one of her moods. There's this thing about the darkness, though, those deep pits of despair. If you weren't careful, you could find yourself falling in, clinging to the edges of the opening, wondering, "How can I get out this time?" Like grandmother, like mother, like daughter, ancestral crap. Sure, I was concerned about myself, too. The apple doesn't fall far from the tree. It wasn't just personality traits or disorders that I feared inheriting. The older I get, I see *them* when I look in the mirror. My grandmother's eyes, my mother's eyes — this is a trait we shared. All of them and me with those wide set light blue eyes. I saw them in my reflection. Every. Time. That was where the similarity stopped, at least with myself and my grandmother. However, I did get Mom's blond locks and her fair skin, but now my hair was more blue-black. I took care of that inherited trait with a little help from a Manic Panic box kit. Now, it was up to me to try to make sense of all the mess.

So here I am. Summer before my senior year,

stuck at home, searching, sorting, and pitching when my life should have been late mornings, long days, and bay side sunsets. I had faced the fact that Mom wasn't getting out. She wasn't ever coming home. Yes, if I had to admit it, I felt relief. It was the truth. And now, here I was in her room, in her mess, trying to right things. It felt like I had to live through the pain of growing up with her as a mother all over again.

THEN

When I was born, it was just us, me and Mom, such a young mother barely 19 years old, my bio dad, whom I would eventually call the "sperm donor," out of the picture. Me and mom, us, living in my grandparent's house. My mom was trying to finish college. She'd wanted to be a writer, a famous author, but that was a dream that had passed her by. My grandmother would even charge her to babysit me so she could go to class. Unreal. Ah, that lovely line of The Horrifying Women, looking out for number one. I imagine it was hard. My grandmother, the ignoring mother, and Mother, looking for love, longing for attention and having me, a baby, in the way of her fame. It wasn't too long before Mother met the man who would become my stepdad.

My grandmother took in boarders, other college students. My future Stepdad would come to call on one of the coeds and play with me. One night, said coed was not home, and he asked out Mother. I don't know how long they dated before they got married, but I know I was part of the package. Once they were married, we became an instant family, although Mother took his name and I still had the sperm donor's name, separating me, severing me. Even though I was the catalyst of the union, they always let me know that I was Other. Mother was the star, and little did my stepdad know in the beginning that years would pass and he would never, ever be able to please her. He was also Other. The 'Others' are less than. They don't matter at all.

NOW

My stepdad, too busy with his own life, couldn't have cared less what I did with all Mom's crap. He just wanted that room, the attic, emptied. It was her room anyway. He'd moved into another part of the house years ago. Always working, head down in the thick of it or traveling, both his own ways of escaping and protecting himself. I think he felt relief now, too. You see, nothing was ever good enough for her. Nothing he did, nothing I did, or anything we tried *not* to do. Mom would never be happy. That was a tough pill to swallow. I got it intellectually, but emotionally, yeah, no. You always hoped to be loved for who you were, knowing that you mattered. You hoped things would change. But Mother was miserable. And you know what they say about misery. Her hopes were squashed, so *your* hopes were going to be squashed as well. And love came with conditions like an unattainable reward, always dangled in front of me like a carrot on a stick. We were the ones she hadn't completely pushed away. We were her captive audience, her only company. Hell, we lived here. Now that Mom was away, my stepdad could have moved out, but me as a minor, I think he felt stuck, obligated. And I was stuck, obligated to cleaning up her shit. But that was me, the 'good girl,' starved for attention. I'd always tried to be the 'good girl,' so here I was doing what I thought was right out of some fucked up allegiance.

Going through all of this shit, the physical

things were, of course, bringing up other shit. It was like regressing, going back in time. There were her writings, of course, pages and pages of it. I found old love letters from the one that got away (*That* one dodged a bullet.) Trinkets, bits of jewelry, pressed flowers, corsages from her past. I was an archeologist. I was on a dig, looking for clues. This melancholy, along with the narcissism, it didn't begin with Mom. Oh no. There was a family history. I come from a pretty scary lineage.

There are many hands holding on, trying desperately to control from the grave. I hear their voices, "How can you be happy? No! You can't. How dare you? How dare you be happy when we are so miserable?" The grip is tight. The imagined clenched hands wrapping furiously around my throat. It's so hard to breathe sometimes. Those fingers yanking on my wrists, pulling me, their hold on my feet, detaining me. The family ghosts will not let me be. I wanted separation. And the only way to do it was to keep excavating, bringing things to the light. I thought I had to relive all this. Stay with the pain. Work through the pain. Crap. I was sounding as dramatic as Mother. The deeper I went into her drawers, her boxes of crap, the deeper I went into my mind.

"Elia, you're late. It's after 10, kid!" The voice of my stepdad broke my stupor. Shit! Fuck! Just like the cinder gal, I'd stayed too late, *not* having the time of my life. Shit. Shit. Shit. I had to get to my summer school class.

I left Mom's attic refuge. Quickly, I put on one of my favorite knee length black dresses, ran a brush through my hair, and slapped on a little sunscreen. Summer in the south — wearing black — not the smartest choice, but SPF 30 was a necessity, so I wouldn't fry. Lastly, I pulled on my secondhand Docs, made of much studier stuff than glass slippers. I'd promised to meet Trudy before class, so I needed to bolt. Trudy and I had been friends for a few years. She was my T. T was my bestie. We were heading into our senior year. Failing the same World History class our junior year, we'd been forced into mandated summer course work in order to join our peers for the last year of this shitshow. It wasn't like we'd skipped too many classes or were vaping in the bathroom stalls. Mostly, we were what you'd call good kids; we'd just been way too busy, holed up at Trudy's house, listening to music and drawing on our tablets, too busy to bother with completing many assignments. We were in our own little world, and I'd needed this world, this escape. T had saved me. Saved me from Mother.

Over the years, Trudy had been my witness, lived through the things I'd lived through, seen the way I was so fucked up because of my mom. She'd been my listening ear, my shoulder to cry on. T had been around for my stepdad's vanishing acts. He was like a ghost himself at times but not like a cool ghost in the attic. She'd seen all the highs and lows and had a front row seat to the rollercoaster ride, which was my adolescence. She knew I wasn't crazy. It was Mother. She was crazy, not me, right? I'd hoped.

We didn't live far from the school. Our town like any other snowbird city. A place where Northerners and retirees flocked in the winters. Quaint houses with picket fences nestled on oak lined streets. Kids playing in yards. Dogs napping on front porches. A place where people ran down to the water's edge at day's end to catch that big yellow ball sinking into the bay. Down south, not far from the coast, always a hint of a salt breeze coming off the water. We'd meet at the intersection of Myrtle Lane and Bay Breeze Way, halfway from my house, halfway from hers, in the middle. It was at those times, the times when I'd see her smiling on her way to meet me, that I felt I'd done my own disappearing act. My house, literally and figuratively, behind me. My friend T, she brought light into my shadows. It's like I'd stepped out of a bad dream every time I left the house. It was like…magic. You know what they say, "People don't know what goes on behind closed doors." Sure, this little beach town looks like a postcard, but you never knew what was lurking, what was going on inside these clapboard cottages. All sunshine on the outside, but inside could be a dark place of pain, and I was living in my own house of emotional terror.

T was my lifeline. There were times, though, I felt the ghosts of my girlhood lingering by our mailbox, and I'd feel like looking over my shoulder, but I couldn't. I knew they'd be there waiting for me when I got home. I'd make the trek back inside, back into the shadows, ready for the wild ride that was my home life. But now it was different. Yes, there was still T. And I still felt the familial phantoms floating around back there, waiting.

And now that Mom was away. I felt a little lighter, but...but... those fingers. I still felt those fingers, like a restraint, like an ankle monitor. I fought their resistance to get that brief probation. After all, I'd been a 'good girl.' I deserved a break.

THEN
The 'good girl,' the pleaser, the glue, whatever you want to call it, that was me, the role I played. When I was about 9 years old, I thought I had a pretty good life. I didn't know any different. Sure, there were those times my mother had bad days, the days of no showers, sweatpants, and wild hair, but didn't everybody's mother have bad days? There were those cheesecake days. The cheesecake days preceded the Xanax years. Mother and my stepdad weren't drinkers, but we all had our vices, what we used to escape when times were tough. My stepdad disappeared into books or work. Mom inhaled entire cheesecakes and me, I cleaned, emptied drawers, moved furniture around, always trying to right things control my surroundings. I think even though I associated my mom with the Cinderella story, her being the Princess, feeling neglected and forgotten, waiting

to be rescued, there was this Queen complex, too.

The Queen wants to rule. The Queen is always right and demands perfection. It's her way or else. You could strive for perfection, try to play by the rules, fit into the picture of the ideal family, only to find out you weren't enough, and then the bar would be set higher. Like a trained poodle, I'd jump through hoops. Like a mouse in a maze, I'd turn myself this way and that, looking for the reward. It was a heavy burden. I was just a little kid, wanting to be loved and not wanting to prove my allegiance to get it. It would be years later that I would see my family life for what it was and see how it was so fucked up. When I was 9, though, I thought this was normal and that everybody lived this way.

CHAPTER 2

NOW

    T was waiting for me. Glancing up from her phone, smiling as usual. I exhaled. There she was, a vision in candy-colored summer wear. T always planned her wardrobe around some kind of theme and had a penchant for decade dressing. It was a little game I played with myself—trying to guess the motivation behind her choices. Today, she looked like a 1980s preppie ice cream sundae: a short white skirt, a pink polo shirt, a mocha sweater tied around her hips and a mint green headband. With her long red hair and sun kissed skin, she was always pretty in pink.

    "Thanks for waiting," I said. "I got caught up in Mom's tower of terror sorting through the bullshit. My life's work, huh?"

"It's ok, Elia," T said as she drew me towards her. And then I got the first dose of my daily hugs. That was the great thing about Trudy. Things were always okay, and I needed someplace in my life to always be okay. We walked the rest of the way to school together, side by side. T was my sidekick, like my better half, and I was better with her. When we first met in the early years, T only came over to my house one time. She wasn't comfortable around the dysfunction. For me, I'd been around it for years. I thought it was normal. I thought that all moms were like mine. It took Trudy coming in from a *normal* home to help me understand that, no, no, this was not a *normal* situation. She began to invite me over to her house for dinner, to do homework, to just vibe. Their house was filled with light and music. It was charmingly Southern and delightfully eclectic — well-loved pieces of antique furniture, passed down from one generation to the next, large works of local art displayed, providing pops of color here and there, and silver-framed family photos atop all the surfaces. Her mom was nice, kind, happy. Her dad told dad jokes. Her parents seemed to actually like each other. And T.

And me. This was all so foreign to me, and it was after meeting her family that I began to realize that my home life was not normal. Our home had that Southern style, too, but it was drab neutral. Most of the time dark, the curtains drawn. There was no art to speak of, and all of our family photos were buried in boxes in Mom's attic room.

Everybody didn't live with a father figure who was either physically missing or verbally silent. Everybody didn't live with a mother who disappeared into desserts, cried in the corner, bellowed from the kitchen, or withdrew into the darkness of her attic bedroom. Every kid was not the glue, trying desperately to hold the family unit together, obediently following rules, doing chores, making the honor roll, the kid who was hoping for peace and love. Every kid did not exist solely to validate the existence of her Mother.

At T's house, though, for me, it was like landing on another planet, being immersed in another culture. I had to learn the language, assimilate, not raise too many red flags, and dial down the crazy. Living in my house, I'd learned to be a master of disguise, walked on eggshells, and didn't want to upset Mother. It wasn't too difficult.

T's home became my home away from Hell. Here, I was liked. Here, there was peace. And I didn't want to fuck it up.

Summer school wasn't too painful. We had the same teacher we'd had for our junior year. Heck, we really were only behind a few papers. And we liked this teacher. We'd have those grades pulled up in no time, and then we'd be ready, ready for our last year of high school. Truthfully, I hated that I'd needed to go to summer school. It was the pleaser in me, the 'good girl.' I *had* to get that grade up. Time in the class seemed to fly by, and around lunchtime, it was time to head out. T and I had papers to work on. We headed over to T's house, raided the fridge and went up to her room.

We had three papers to write and a month and a half to write them. At least the subject matter was cool. We were studying ancient civilizations and female deities. T was going with Hindu Goddesses, and I was thinking about Greece, Hera, Athena, Persephone, you know, protectors, warriors, mother archetypes I could get down with. But it was Persephone that I fell in love with. If my mom identified with the cinder gal, the princess waiting to be rescued, I associated my life with Persephone, destined to live between the dark and the light, looking for protection and love, innocent and damned.

I'd researched some about the Greek goddess Persephone, and I'd gotten the gist: daughter of Demeter and Zeus, bride of Hades. And I'll tell you why I felt the feels for this story. Demeter, also known as "The Mother," so loved Persephone, protected her in a Mommie Dearest kind of way, believed that no guy would ever be good enough for her baby girl. But Hades, he wanted Persephone down under. He tricked her with the narcissus flower (symbolizing early death), and basically, when she reached for it, the earth opened up, and she plummeted into the bowels of Hell. Mommy Dearest was not having that. Her darling daughter could not be living in the land of the lost souls as the Queen of the Dead. I mean, come on. Persephone's only company could not be these corpses or ghosts day in and day out, right? Big fight between Demeter and Hades. Zeus gets sick of this and wants things settled. There's something about a pomegranate in here and more trickery by Hades.

I can just see Persephone...yes, ok, the story goes she just ate a few seeds, but I envision this bulbous fruit, her taking large bites, red, juicy, pulpy, like blood and viscera, dripping down my split-apart's chin. I imagine she's been down there for a while and was hungry, ravenous. But I digress. Anyway, Zeus decided that Persephone would spend half the year in Hell and half of the year with her mother. Mic drop Zeus. The Greeks use this myth to explain the change of seasons, representing the cycle of death and rebirth. But I'm like, hey, at least she got six months of the year away from her mom, right? And ghosts don't make *too* bad of friends.

Yeah. I'd gotten the main points of this myth down, but I needed more information. Something a little more than the same old story. Something that would make my research more interesting. T was having trouble, too. Her Google searches came up with not much on Saraswati, another Mother Goddess not unlike Demeter, just from another place on the map. After working on the outlines for our papers, we decided to head downtown to our local witchy head shop, *Mystic Blue*, home of all things needed for otherworldly interests and pursuits. The kind of shop haunted by the local sulky teenagers with strong b.o. masked in patchouli and cloves who wore only dark Emo garb, even in the dead of summer in the south, with the occasional spiked collar. Their hair was often a shock of some experimental shade that shifted week to week. They may offer you a darting glance through kohl rimmed eyes. They rarely purchased anything from *Blue*, mostly just taking up space on the sidewalk out front. Then, there were the gray headed mamas smelling like essential oils and a hint of weed donning long flowing tie-dyed gypsy skirts fancying themselves akin to the white witch, Miss Stevie Nicks. They kept *Blue* in business as they were of the age when you were trying to figure out everything you'd done wrong in your life thus far in order to reinvent yourself for your next chapter. It was kind of store the little old ladies skirted by clutching their pearls or crossing themselves, hoping if they passed the shop entrance quickly enough that maybe the devil wouldn't get 'em. You know, where you could get your cards read, schedule a past life regression session, pick up some crystals, or buy some rolling papers. And books. They had loads of books, all the kinds you would think you'd find in a store like this. Books on meditation, alien abduction, self-help, spell work, the occult, and, of course, they'd have something on goddesses, what with us living in a time that was ripe for taking down the patriarchy.

After eating lunch and scrolling on our screens for a while, we left Trudy's house and continued down her street, Bay Breeze Way, towards the downtown shops. If you hadn't lived here your whole life, it didn't look like a bad place to live. Sunny days and mild winters, it was appealing to some. But if you'd grown up here, like anywhere else, I guess, you wanted to get out, see more of the world. Mom had never gotten out, which is probably why she created these alternate worlds for herself, first in our home, then in her writing and when the walls closed in there, at The Spa. She needed the escape. The older Mom got, though, the more trouble she had coming back to any semblance of reality, just stayed in the make believe, and we couldn't reach her, the Xanax trip that never ended. Well, except for when she'd skip a dose. Then we got the bear. She seemed happier on the Xanax, though. The Xanax days were the Real Housewives days: blond hair just so, make up on point, impeccably dressed, and accessorized — a reality television star on the show in her head. Yes, she seemed happier on these days. I know my stepdad and I were. We could breathe a little easier. Still, it was like coming back from the war. We were shell shocked. And we never knew when we might set off a grenade.

It was about that time that I glanced over at my friend. The sun hitting T's smiling face, eyes a bit squinty in the light, glints of gold bouncing off her auburn tresses. I had to smile to myself then. You couldn't help it around T. She rubbed off on you in a good way. She looked at me about that time, too, and grabbed my hand, swinging along as we walked towards *Mystic Blue*.

"I know summer school is a bummer," T said, "but I'm glad we're in it together."

"Yeah. I know. Makes it more bearable."

"I hope we can find what we need and get more information for our research. Maybe we'll find enough for all three papers. It would be great to finish up early, before the end of July."

"I know, right?" Yeah. It would be cool to finish up summer school and get a break before senior year started in August. But *then* what was

I going to do? I'd have no excuse then to finish going through my mom's stuff and clear that room out. Maybe it's exactly what I needed, though. No excuses. Get rid of her shit and move on. Yeah. Maybe that's exactly what I needed.

"Hey T. What if we looked into some spell stuff while we're at *Mystic Blue*? They might have just what I need to help me get past all the bullshit with Mom, close the door on all that, ya know? Wooooo," I said, coming at T, my eyes wide, wiggling my fingers in the air. T looked at me sideways and then down at her feet.

"I don't know," T said. "Should we really get into that? Sounds kind of dark." She looked up at me with questioning eyes, eyes that looked greener outside in the sun. That was T. Always looking for the light.

"No, no," I countered, waving my hands. "It's not like that at all. Yes, it would be like a ritual sort of, but this stuff is everywhere now, even in Cosmo and shit like that." Witchcraft is more accepted, more mainstream, trendy even. Although they aren't calling it Witchcraft anymore. You see words more like 'manifest' or 'vision statement,' stuff like that. But still, no matter what kind of bow you wrapped it in or rather what whimsical font was typed across the glossy page next to a photo of a girl with abnormally pumped-up lips and gravity defying breasts stirring her cauldron, it was still craft work. I just wouldn't mention that part to T.

Here we were, 1326 Bay Breeze Way, home of *Mystic Blue*, the southern shop meeting all your witchy, er, metaphysical needs. No matter how mainstream this kind of stuff had become, a southern beach town was only going to let you get away with so much before the Baptists protested with signs and crap like "Save your children's souls!" or "What is happening in your own neighborhood?" Then, the doors would have to close. So yeah, it's our little metaphysical shop.

We walked in still hand in hand, the "Namaste Y'all" sign flapping against the glass with the opening of the door, bells ringing above our head, blessed AC blowing, new age music playing, the smell of incense greeting us as if to say, "Come. Join us." Every time I entered *Mystic Blue*, I felt those ghost fingers that usually held me so tight let go, the phantoms fading into the street. They didn't like it in *Blue*. This place was special.

Besides T's house, this is where I felt at home, less stressed. We let go of hands and split off into different directions. T cut right to the bookshelves, staying on track. I headed this way and that, tables of jewelry and crystals all throughout the shop, tapestries on the walls, dream catchers hanging from the ceiling, and then I was greeted by my favorite green-haired, tattooed adult. Today, that green mass was piled atop her head in a makeshift bun, some tendrils sticking to her neck either because the massage room was warmer than the rest of the shop or the oils she used in her work were gluing them in place like tiny snakes wrapping round her neck. Kelly was just coming out of the back finishing up a massage, bare feet, bliss, and soft smiles. Kelly was one of the younger "Woo Woo Girls" in town, those spiritual, new-age, witchy, ghost hunting, full moon following tribe of wonderful women. There's a group of 'em in every town.

"Hey, Elia," Kelly said, hugging me, another of the hug fixes I needed. "I've just finished with a client, and I don't have anyone scheduled for another hour or so. What's up? Looking for anything special today?"

She lit some sage and began to smudge, leaving trails of smoke that hung in the air as she walked this way and that, making figure 8s around the shop. Kelly was at least a head taller than I was. Her magenta top sliding off of one shoulder. I guessed she was showing off her Hawaiian Tropic glow. Looking into those hazel cat-like eyes that tipped up at the corners, I said, "T and I are in summer school (I made a noose around the neck yank motion), taking World History and writing papers on ancient civilizations and goddesses. We thought we'd come to *Blue* and look for some books that might help. T is working on Saraswati, and I've got Persephone."

"Ooooo," Kelly crooned and then paused a second. "But that can't be all you came in for today, is it? Looking for a bit of the *wooooo*?" And she moved towards me, smirking, waving her gemstone bejeweled fingers in the air. Either Kelly was super intuitive, or I just came in here too damn much.

"Well, actually," I started, "I have been thinking about, oh, I don't know, maybe doing some spell work?"

"Ah," Kelly closed her eyes and nodded,

"I thought so. I could just sense it, you know?" Then she wiggled her fingers in my face again and laughed that kind of laugh that comes across as quiet and internal, shoulders slightly shaking. "Let's go up to the front of the store where T is, and we can look through the books, yes?"

"Oh, about that," I said, "T is not too cool with spell work. She's a little spooked by the whole idea. So, let's use words like "intention" or "goal setting." K?"

Kelly winked, "Gotcha." Then she turned towards the nearest table, put her sage out in an abalone shell and twirled, her skirt of many colors fanning out like a cloud, heading to the storefront.

Trudy saw us coming. She untied her sweater and pulled it over her head, adjusting her headband. Either the AC was getting to her, or she was insulating herself with a barrier. T was never quite sure what would happen on our visits to *Blue*. She liked Kelly, but she was uneasy around most of the "Woo Woo Girls" in town. After all, they were quite a force if you encountered them all together. Shit. I liked them. Those women were fierce! T's face brightened, and she and Kelly shared a warm hug.

"What's up, T? Elia here tells me you two are working on research for Ancient Civilizations," Kelly offered. "I think I have something…" And she bent down to the lowest shelf and pulled out a book on world religions, handing it to T. "Here you go, T. I think this may be just what you need. Elia said your Goddess was Saraswati, right? You'll find useful information in the chapters on Hinduism. Now, Elia…you were looking for a couple of things, right? Something for class and something for, what was it, *goal setting*?"

T shot me a questioning look, and her eyes, grayer when inside, bored through me for a second. Then, she nodded a thanks to Kelly and wandered off to thumb through her book, always able to stay focused. Kelly grabbed a book on Greek Myth, handed it to me and said, "Now, let's go to the back hall behind the hippy curtain and see what we may see."

I headed to the back with Kelly glancing over my shoulder at T. She'd found a comfy beanbag and had her nose stuck in the world religion book, not even noticing we'd moved. I followed Kelly through the Boho beads, past the bathroom and to what I thought was just a tapestry hung on the wall where the hall ended. Kelly moved the wall hanging to the side, and there were shelves, floor to ceiling, with more books, bottles, packages of incense, jars of herbs, tongue of frog, eye of newt, the witchy stuff, tucked away from the prying eyes of the ladies-who-lunch type.

Kelly looked left and right, up and down, finally, her fingertips landing on a well-worn hardback book. She took the book, blew off some dust and handed it to me. "Ah," she said, "This book has helped me in the past, but it's been a while since I've used it. Take it home, look it over for a couple of days and see what speaks to you."

"I'm looking for a spell for getting rid of something, letting go of some shit, you know?"

Then, Kelly reached out her hand, placing it on my shoulder. She closed her eyes and nodded slowly, solemnly saying, "Oh yes. I know." Then, she laughed that quiet laugh again, spun around to leave the hall, but quickly turned back. "Once you find what you're looking for, come back after hours on Thursday with the book. We'll be having a *gathering,* and all the Girls will be here. We'll make sure you have what you need to perform your spell. I mean, *set your goals.* Wink." Her top had made its way back over her shoulder. Kelly gave it a tug down, freeing the inked moth on the top of her copper skinned back and, with an actual wink of an almond eye, disappeared back into the shop.

CHAPTER 3

Trudy and I made our purchases, and I slipped the other book from the back into my bag with my stuff. I thought I'd been sly, but T saw me acting sketch. Once we were out on the sidewalk and about a block from *Blue*, T stopped walking and faced me head on. "Ok, Elia. What's in the bag?" She may not have really wanted to be involved in any kind of spell work or ritual, but she was direct.

"Oh, another book Kelly loaned me," I said. "I didn't think you'd be interested because, you know, witchy stuff, dark shit."

"Yes, I know I said that, but… I am curious, and you are my bestie." T didn't want to be left out, weird shit, my family shit, school shit, magic shit. It didn't matter in the end. I should have known better.

"Ok, ok. I told Kelly I wanted to find a ridding spell to help me let go of my mom's stuff so I could loosen her hold on me." I hoped that was what it would do anyway. "So, she took me in the back and…"

"Elia!" T scolded, "You know that's where all the suspect crap is! The items they hide away from the general public." The general public was T's nice way of referring to the pearl wearing Bible thumpers.

"I know," I said. "But I really, really want to do this! I need to do this. I don't know how much longer I can live with the trauma, my mom's trauma. It trickles down, you know. From my mom, my grandmother, and who knows how many others are linked in my family chain. I just want to feel lighter, feel happy. And I know, from years spent in the school's counseling office off and on, that my misery is mostly of my own making. I allow it. I'm not stupid. But I have to break the bonds. I just want a little help, a visual, something to do. Please do this with me? Please."

"Oh, alright," T said.

"Yay!" I may have squealed a little as I gave

her a big squeeze. Hell, that was a breakthrough in itself. I hardly ever initiated physical contact. "Ok, ok. Kelly said to look in the book, find what I'm interested in, and come back Thursday night when the "Woo Woo Girls" meet, and they'll help me get whatever I need."

"Wait, what?" T said. Shit. I knew this part would be the hard part. "You know how I feel about those Girls. They freak me out a little." T was acting dodgy, and I felt her about to pull out of this.

"Aw, c'mon," I said. "Most of them are over 65, for fuck's sake. Can't you think of them as kindly grandmothers?"

"Oh, like *your* grandmother Elia?"

Fair point. She had me there.

T sighed, "Alright. I'll do it. Now, let's go back to my house, skip the homework for a while and look in the book. Is there some index or something, you know, like a list or a guide with things like 'Find True Love,' 'Create Riches Beyond Your Wildest Dreams,' 'Off Your Meddlesome Neighbor'?" Then, Trudy, pursing her lips and rolling her eyes skyward, leaned in and wiggled her fingers near my face. And I knew she was in.

Back at Trudy's house, we were ready to grab a couple of sodas from the kitchen but then thought, no, hot tea, all the better to create a witchcore aesthetic, set the mood. Once in T's room, mugs of peppermint tea steaming on a side table, we tossed our bags on the floor, sprawled out on T's bed, ready to look in the book. "Gosh," T said, "It seems pretty old. What's the copyright?"

I flipped to the front, blank. "Huh," I said, "No publishing date, no publisher." I turned to the back of the book. Nothing here either save cursive writing, scribblings, notes taken by other Girls before us, I guessed.

T squinted at the scrawl, "How did they ever learn to read that, much less write that way?"

Me, I'd seen it and worked on deciphering it for years. That's the form I usually found all my mom's musings and ramblings written. "That was a different time, T before everyone used their thumbs to communicate," I said, jokingly and gently nudging her in the side.

Lying on our bellies side by side, heads together, we began to turn page by yellowed page carefully. They were so brittle. There was so much to go through. This book had to have been at least

500 pages, maybe more. After about half an hour, I realized the book was divided by moon phases. "Ok. Look T. There are sections, some kind of order to this woo woo."

"Yes, I see, but how do we know when this *intention* should be performed?" She couldn't say spell, but she was standing by me, so I wasn't going to correct her.

"Well," I said, "If I'm wanting to get rid of something, have less of something, maybe the moon should be in a stage of waning?" My mother had been somewhat into astrology, so I was no slouch when it came to the planets and the stars. I had learned the hard way what Mercury in retrograde meant. Be extra careful around Mother, lie low, duck and cover, is what that meant. T looked at me, blinking, lost, shrugging her shoulders. Anyway, I found the waning moon section. "Ok," I said, "Now we are on to something!" A few pages into that section and I exclaimed, "Fuck yeah! Here we go!" I read on: "Letting Go, Making Space, Cutting Cords to Past Relationships. T, this is it!"

{*Cutting Cords to Past Relationships: The best time to perform this spell is under the waning cycle of the moon, sometimes referred to as waning gibbous or waning crescent. In this moon phase, the size of the moon is decreasing, so it is the perfect time to practice letting go, releasing what no longer serves you, or any kind of cutting ritual.}*

Ouch. Ok. That hit a little close to home. I had a history of cutting. It was a way I'd coped with negative emotions and dealt with relief from bad feelings, or so the school counselor said. Since Mother was away, most of my bleak baggage had faded into the background, but there were times… Ok, Elia, get your shit together and keep reading. T must have known I'd feel this way reading this, and it was about that time she reached for my hand and offered a small comforting squeeze. Big exhale. I got this.

{This spell can be executed in two ways:

Take three (or the number of things you want to release plus one for yourself) strands of string or yarn, tie a knot in one end. Braid them together. Pull one string out (this strand represents you) and cut this piece away from the other strands, while visualizing yourself walking away from the things you wish to sever from your life.

Make a list of items you'd like to release. Put

pen to paper. Cut the paper into small pieces or strips. Burn all of the pieces. You may want to create a chant to repeat as the papers turn to ash.

*The waning moon is also an ideal time to get a haircut.

End either ritual or spell work by saying, "Aho. It is done."}

We'd found the spell. T was like, "Ooooo. Let's cut our hair too! I like that!"

Again, just another sign, T was in.

"It seems kind of short, the spell, vague even. Kelly said I'd need to come back on Thursday night when the Girls were there, and they would help me. But we can at least make a list of what we think we need so I look a little prepared." Me. The 'good girl' wanting credit for doing homework even if the homework was spell work. Hungry for praise. "Which one should I focus on?"

"I like the burning one," T said. There was something about redheads and fire.

I agreed. "That's good, I think. I can use my mom's papers, too, make it really personal. And I think I saw some large shears in her room the last time I was up there going through her shit."

Now it was time to put pen to paper, write everything down, make a list. It was Tuesday. The full moon was in a couple of days. Fuck, of course, it was. That's why the Girls were meeting this week. Waning moon was next. I wouldn't have long to wait. Time to set the spell work aside, though, and get onto the homework. Two days. Big exhale again. I got this.

CHAPTER 4

I needed to head home before dark. The fingers had loosened their grip and let me go for a while today. It had been a pretty good day, but the darker it got and the closer I got to home, the familiar grip, the pull, the fingers found their way back to me. As I approached my front door, the heaviness returned. I felt weighted. The joy of the day behind me. I went in and gave a '*sup* nod to my silent Stepdad, his head stuck in a book.

Heading up the stairs, each step felt like I was sinking in quicksand. I'd had a nice day-cation today, and now it was time to get back to it. I was always caught somewhere in the middle, taking on adult responsibilities at home and getting to be a normal teenager with T. I tossed my things on the floor in the hall outside her door. My things. My things staying on the outside. It was never about me. As I entered Mom's room, her hold on me felt tighter than ever. Even though she wasn't here, she was *here*.

I decided to focus on one box. I didn't remember ever looking in this one. I opened the top flaps, looked inside, and, of course, it was full of more papers. More of her writings and ramblings, her wordplay, incoherent. The thousands of words a reminder of when she slipped away from reality and went somewhere else. You know, for the most part, it was extremely difficult being raised by Mother, but as I got older, I began to see the other side of things. I knew truly little about my grandmother, but I knew growing up with her — for my mom and her sister — must have been a real shit show.

With each generation, the toll was taken, the fingers holding so firmly. The matriarch of each generation wanting control so badly! Way back when, my grandmother had been the queen, the center of it all, making my mom and my aunt feel less than the ones that didn't matter — Other. So, my mom grew up as the princess in her own mind, wanting to be rescued, hoping the slipper would fit and she could find her happily ever after. My aunt took off at 18, escaping. They never saw each other after that. One day a few years ago, Mom received news of her sister's death in a certified letter, but she never talked about it. Stuff the pain down and carry on. Mother teetered on the edge of insanity, and then when I came along, a new queen emerged as there was a new princess to boss around, me, only I felt like a lady in waiting most of the time. Mother exerting her control, wanting to have things her way, wanting things to be perfect.

Page after page after page, damn, she wrote and wrote and wrote. I guess she was trying to write her way back to the real world or maybe writing and writing and writing to extend her stay in the surreal. All of these papers, pages, notebook after notebook, I felt like I was drowning in them. I felt like I was drowning underneath the thousands of words my mother wrote. She was always writing, trying to make sense of her life. I almost felt sorry for her. Almost.

THEN

When I was about 10 years old, maybe I

was in the 5th grade, Mom had surgery. It wasn't her first, and it wouldn't be her last. I can't even remember the first time I'd been in a hospital waiting room. My mom's side of the family *loved* to go to the hospital. One of the few memories I have of my grandmother was going to the hospital. I'd be sound asleep in my bed, and Mom would come and wake me up in the middle of the night. "Get up," she would say, "Your grandmother has called an ambulance to take her to the hospital." And we'd get dressed and go. The funny thing is I don't remember there ever being anything terribly wrong. I did know that my grandmother loved to ride in ambulances and talk to the paramedics. She was, after all, the star.

So, whatever Mom's surgery was that time, I remember her coming home, and this bell, this cream-colored bell with brown flowers etched on it, appeared on her bedside table. Ring, ring, ring. She would ring that bell whenever she needed something. And you're thinking, "Of course she would. People recovering from surgery need assistance." And you'd be right, but the bell stayed. Months, years after, she would continue to ring that fucking bell from her bed, signaling for either me or my stepdad to come to her and see what she needed. The queen coming into her full power. I'm not sure what eventually happened to the bell; one day, it wasn't there anymore. Maybe it got broken accidentally. Yeah, accidentally.

NOW

Ugh. Daylight was making its way through the blinds. I had no idea what time it was. I must have fallen asleep on the floor going through my mom's shit, taking my mental trip down memory lane. Crap. Nothing like lying on a hard floor. The women in my family robbing me of a good night's sleep.

It was early. I had a few hours before summer school. I organized her piles and boxes the best I could, creating some kind of order. Follow the rules. Do as you're told. The 'good girl' making things right. The more I went through her things, her writing, her clothes, her memories tucked away, the more I could understand her. I mean, well shit, I, too, knew what it was like to have a narcissistic mother, didn't I? And yes, I felt sorry for her. That's part of the programming. *Your* feelings don't matter. And the guilt, the manipulation. That was the end goal, piling so much on the underling, in this case, the daughter, that you would never leave, could never leave. This is why I had to do the spell. Years of counseling hadn't helped much. I needed something else. I had to let all of this go, the lying, the control, the guilt. I wanted happiness. I was almost 18. I wanted more control of my adult life. And I couldn't get it emotionally tethered to this house, to the ancestors, all of the women who came before me. I had to break the chain, leave these old ghosts behind. Yeah, I felt bad for Mother. I felt bad for all of us. Them and me.

I was just about to leave her room when I thought, "Oh shit. I've got to grab a couple of things before I meet T today." I went back to the boxes, reached in the first one I saw, and picked up the pages on the top. Never mind what they were. Did it matter? I figured any of her writing would work, would represent her, the stuff I needed to cut out of my life for the spell work. I glanced quickly at the heading, my mom's words, "The Mother Who Never Loved Me." Yup. We were all in this together, after all. Then, I went to her dressing table and opened a side drawer. Her crafting scissors,

yes, those would work. I had to laugh to myself.
Crafting scissors. No way in hell would Mother
use those for witch 'craft,' but I would! Papers in
one hand, I closed the drawer holding the shears
in the other. Crap. I'd nicked myself trying to do
too many things at once. I quickly put my finger
between my lips. Shit. Shit. Shit. As I closed the
door to her room, I looked down. I'd gotten some
blood on the papers. Oh well, it couldn't hurt, I
guess.

I hurriedly got dressed, i.e., threw on
something black. Had my bag, my stuff and myself
ready. My stepdad was nowhere to be seen. I
headed out to meet Trudy at our spot. I saw her
coming my way. Ah. Today was a retro day, circa
1970s. T had on ragged cut-offs, a bright as the sun
yellow halter top, love beads round her neck and
daisies in her hair. As usual, I instantly felt lighter,
freer. Got my morning hug and felt the ghosts let
go.

"Hey T, I got the stuff!"

"Stuff?" T said.

"Yeah, the stuff we need for the waning
moon spell, you know?" I replied with a small
wiggle of my fingers.

"Slay!" Then, T spotted the dried blood on my right index finger. "Uh, what is that?"

"Oh, that's just my blood. I was farting around, trying to do too much at once and *snip*. You know, T, I'm always an accident waiting to happen." That got me my second hug of the day.

"I got some of Mom's writing AND her crafting scissors."

"Ooooo. Cool. Let's start with the haircuts today after class. Cut. Cut. Cut," T said while making hacking motions with her fingers.

After class, we walked to T's house. We grabbed snacks from the pantry. I was starving. I guess I'd forgotten to eat today. Plus, T's mom always had good shit to eat. Our kitchen was usually bare. My stepdad ate out a lot, and neither one of us were the domestic type. In fact, I don't think anyone had cooked a proper meal at our house in years. When Mom had cooked, it was such a production, like she was putting on a show. She wanted the credit. Her meals seemed to scream, "Look what I've done for you!" After dining on some kind of broiled meat, some kind of boiled vegetable, and some kind of burnt bread, she repeatedly asked us if it was good, if the food was ok. Most of the time, it was frickin bland, but we placated her. She needed the praise, the recognition. It was kind of sad, and it wasn't until years later that I realized how weird it was that she asked us over and over again until she felt it.

Up in T's room, we spread out all our stuff and worked on our papers. The first ones were due by the end of this week, and they were coming along. Next week, we'd be onto more old religion goddess stuff—not a bad way to spend your summer vacation.

"I'm about done with Saraswati," T said.

"I'm getting close to finishing, too," I shot back.

"So…let's put our schoolwork away and get to the spell, er, I mean intention work." Oh, T was so in!

"It's too soon to do the actual work, T," I said. "We have to wait, you know, 'til the moon is waning, and we meet with the Girls tomorrow night."

"WE?" T asked.

Uh oh. Was T chickening out? "I thought you were ok with this, all of this?" I asked.

"I'm okay with most of this, but those

women, those *Girls*, they worry me."

"It will be fine, T. Kelly would never get me into something shady. It's cool."

"Ugh," T sighed, "Alright. I'm all in. Now, about the haircuts." T seemed really ready for this!

"Ah. I don't know T. It's just reaching full moon. The moon won't be waning til the weekend."

"Well," T said, "I need a summer 'do. I'm ready NOW. Let's break in your Mom's scissors."

"Oh well. Couldn't hurt, I guess." I gave in. Always a pleaser.

We stood side by side, looking into T's vanity mirror in her bathroom, scissors on the counter. Me, my raven cropped locks brushing my shoulders, cornflower blue eyes staring back at me. T, a little bit shorter than I was, her long reddish hair halfway down her back with some layers framing her face and those grey green eyes, more grey than green inside. She looked cute, sassy. I hated to see her chop it off. With that, she took the flowers out of her hair and bent over, putting it all in a ponytail holder, flipped up right, took one look at me, grinning from ear to ear, grabbed my Mom's shears and WHACK. That was it. Ponytail gone!

I stood frozen for a minute. Then T reared back and let out a huge laugh. "I love it!" she squealed.

"Me too!" I said.

Her hair, now just skimming her jawline, fell nicely into a bob. T turned to me, "Now, your turn. Cut. Cut. Cut." And with that, I began to saw at the straight edges. It was fun. It was reckless. It was familiar.

THEN

I started cutting at about 12 or 13 years old. The years when my mom was still living with us were tough. Whether it was playing the role of the glue for her marriage, tip-toeing around trying not to set her off, trying to be perfect, or answering the call of that damn bell, it wore on me. That's a lot of pressure to put on a kid. Me, the kid, feeling responsible for Mother's happiness. But that's the role of the child of a narcissistic parent. You are Other. Your feelings don't matter.

I didn't have many close friends, and I certainly never asked anyone to come over to my house. One, Mom was not the greatest at having people over. It was a whole ordeal. Looking back,

I see that my mom never looked forward to the things normal people get excited about, like family dinners, vacations, parties. It was all work and obligation to her. Two, I never knew which Mom I was going to get. Would she be the star, putting on a show for an audience, or would she be in her robe, face puffy and red from crying, coming out of her room only to get more cheesecake?

Then, in middle school, I met Trudy. Trudy was new to our town. I saw her at lunch one day, tray in hand, looking around for a place to sit. I was sitting alone as usual. She headed towards me and sat down. This was before she had stepped fully into her fashion sense, but it must have been close to Halloween because she had on this headband with bats bobbing around on springs hovering over her carrot top. She started talking. I never started conversations as I felt so awkward and undeserving. Then, she smiled. I felt my body soften. And for once, I smiled back. I had a friend.

I went over to Trudy's house on a regular basis. I'd found a home there. Her parents were nice. It was all sugar, smiles, and warmth. Love. The ghosts couldn't get me there. After a few weeks, I finally asked T over to my house. One day after school, we headed down my street instead of hers. I was nervous. I had no idea what was going to happen. Mom was in one of her 'star' moods, though. She was on stage, had a new audience member. I figured it was a Xanax day. Xanax days were usually more tolerable.

Everything was fine until T went home. The door barely shut, my mother turned to me and said, "So, you have a *friend* now. She seems *nice*," ice dripping from her words. "You know, you can't bring her over here again, right? This is our home. It's private. Who knows what she might see or hear, and then she'll tell other people, and everyone will judge me, talk about me? No, that will never do."

And for once, I talked back to her, "Mom, no, I like her! She's my friend. I'm happy when I'm with her." And with that, I'd gone too far.

"Happy?" my mom said, "Happy! There is so much pain in the world, Elia. How can you be happy? People are suffering. I'm suffering. You think she's your *friend?* She'll only talk about you behind your back, end up leaving you. And then where will you be? Back here with *me.* No. I'll not have it. Why do you think she likes *you* anyway?

You're nobody special." She looked at me like she hated me. "Elia, you are not to bring her over here anymore, understand?" I nodded, my eyes filling with tears. "Good. Do as you're told, Elia, and life will be easier," she said over her shoulder as she was walking, heading up to her attic room, her fortress of insanity.

And that's how it started. I shut down. I felt numb. T was the only friend I'd ever had, much less invited over to my house. It was later that night, alone in my room, when I first cut myself. I wanted to feel something, anything other than the pain of living with my mother. The first time, it hurt like hell. The first time, it was just the tip of my finger with an Exacto knife I'd been using in art class. I gasped, immediately bringing my fingertip to my mouth. It tasted metallic, like when you pop a fresh piece of gum from foil, and you accidentally bite down on some of the wrapper. Familiar but different. Then I did it again. And again.

I switched from my finger to my inner thighs, not wanting to draw attention to myself. I was used to shrinking. If Mom saw these cuts, well, I'd be stealing the spotlight, wouldn't I? Even at that age, I knew better than that! My whack-job

Mom would probably start cutting herself, too. Competition was fierce with her. I kept doing it in private. The cutting was the only thing that brought me out of my desensitized haze. I felt something. I felt more in control. So, I kept on for a while.

A couple of days went by, and then one day at school, Trudy came up to me donning a sequined holiday sweater and was like, "What's going on? Why have you been ignoring me? Did I do something?

"No, no," I said. "Just some stuff going on at home with Mom."

"Oh," T said, brightening. "Your mom seemed…nice."

People on the outside always thought this. Little by little, T would discover the truth about my home life. Of course, Xanax always made people seem nice.

"Ok. Good!" she said and then leaned in a gave me a big hug. I didn't know what to do. I stood there frozen. T pulled back and smiled, "I'm a hugger." I attempted to smile back. This was the first of my daily T hugs, and God knows I needed them. That was T, though. She was loyal. She didn't want to be left out. I needed that, too. In retrospect,

I knew my mom couldn't keep me from seeing T all the time, but as a kid, I gave away my power. It was time to get it all back.

NOW

I looked at T and looked back at the mirror. I didn't feel anxious or down. Instead, I started to laugh. "Holy Shit, T! Look what I've done to my fucking hair!" T hesitated (I knew what she was thinking about, that we'd fucked up and triggered something in me, and I was really losing it), but after a few seconds, she started to laugh with me.

"Ok," she said, picking at the jagged pieces of my hair, "We can do something with this." I hacked at it a little more, and T got out some product. We slicked back the sides behind my ears and fluffed up the top a bit. I'd just call this some kind of sheared, short shag. "Now you need earrings."

Walking out of T's bathroom in a pair of her silver hoops, I noticed that it had gotten dark. "I gotta bolt T. It's getting late. And you know I've got to visit Mother at The Spa tomorrow. Can you turn in my Persephone paper?"

"You know I will, Elia." T gave me a big

hug. God, what would I do without those hugs?

She walked me to her front door, and I was walking through the threshold when I remembered, "T, don't forget about tomorrow night and going to *Blue*, you know, to see the Girls," I said, wiggling my fingers in front of her face as I said, Girls.

"I know, I know," she said, "I remember." Eyeroll T.

As I moved towards the sidewalk, I shot back over my shoulder, "No worries, T. If you get too scared or if one of the ladies gives you the evil eye, I'll just have Kelly smudge the shit outta you," I laughed.

"Oh, ha, ha," T said, turning away, her new bob swinging right to left as she walked inside, closing the door behind her.

On my way home, I couldn't help smiling. Shit, I'd had a good time! I'd laughed. T and I had been partners in crime, with the great hair massacre. I felt happy? These moments of happiness were few and far between and still felt unusual like they didn't quite fit. And I still felt guilty for feeling happy. I carried all that pressure from Mom still. If Mom wasn't happy, then I couldn't be happy. That was the way it was. With that, I sighed, turned the corner, and caught sight of my house. The ghosts were waiting for me, and the closer I got, the tighter their grip, the invisible hands dragging me closer. But only one more day and I'd have the info I needed to release the others, break the chain. Then, the real countdown would begin, waiting for the waning moon.

CHAPTER 5

I woke in my own room, having skipped going into Mom's last night. There wasn't much to it, my room. All of the walls in our house were once white, now dinghy. Between the two houses, T's and mine, I was caught between worlds like Persephone. Light and dark. Life and Death. The best thing about my room, though, was now that Mom was at The Spa, it was all mine. No one forcing their way in and prying. I had privacy now. I got up and took one look in the mirror and was startled for a second. I had serious bed head and then remembered the whacking away of my hair the day before. Taking some water and product, I tried to replicate what T had done yesterday. A little makeup would help. Usually, I skipped it, but I had to wear makeup to see my mom at The Spa today. One of her favorite barbs, "I don't know why you don't wear makeup more often, Elia. It does so much for you." One of those "Is that a compliment or a dig" remarks she was famous for.

It was about time to go. I went downstairs to the kitchen for a cup of coffee. My stepdad was standing there eating cereal, looking tired, shoulders slumped, wearing his conservative "dad" clothes: pinstriped short sleeved button down tucked into khakis with a leather belt and loafers. "Elia, you look different. Oh. Your hair. It looks like it's been run over by a lawnmower. Your Mother is going to have a field day with that." My stepdad had noticed my handiwork.

"T and I sort of gave ourselves makeovers yesterday. It will grow," I said, tugging at it. There I was, making excuses and defending myself and my actions. That was another response, textbook, really. Since you were only an extension of a parent, not an individual, you couldn't have any opinions or original thoughts. When you veered from their idea of *normal,* you were on trial. "Well, Elia. Too late now to do anything about it. Wait 'til your Mother sees it. You better brace yourself." I knew. I was ready.

The drive to The Spa wasn't far. We rode in silence. T and I had always joked that my stepdad had a set word count he could use for the day. I guess with my mom, after so many "Yes dear," patent responses, you just kind of gave up and laid low, lost in your own thoughts. Hell, I never knew where he was mentally or physically most of the time. As we pulled up through the gates, I took it all in. She'd been here what two years now? But I guess since I've gotten older, I was noticing more things about the place. It was weird. There was a heaviness present. It was a perfectly warm, bright day in late June in our little coastal area, and here it felt like October. Clouds had moved in, blocking the sun, the trees on the property barren except for the Spanish moss, which swayed eerily from the ancient oaks. How the moss moved without a hint of a breeze, I don't know. The building was gray, needing repair and a new paint job. The staff, few and far between. It wasn't like a state hospital, I mean state 'spa,' you know, like in *One Flew Over the Cuckoo's Nest*, a 'take all the meds in your paper cup lest you get the hose again' kind of place, but it also wasn't like those other gated places closer into town with all the bells and whistles on the property — doctors, full-time staff, pilates.

As we made our way through the guest check-in, I began to feel short of breath, tense, and like my feet were glued to the floor. The ghosts may have let me go at T's house and at *Blue*, but they liked it here. They were all here, dragging me in against my will as if to say, "Come. Join us." Or maybe it was more like the chant T and I had heard late one Saturday night watching the old movie *Freaks* — "One of us. One of us."

We walked side by side at first, like two old war buddies. The air smelled like piss and antiseptic at the same time. As we got closer to her room, my pace slowed, and I dropped back. I didn't know if I could do it, didn't know if I was up for it today. "You wanna go in first, get it over with, yank the bandage?" my stepdad asked. I don't think he was looking forward to this visit either. But as the war buddies, the victims, we'd been groomed. We felt a sick loyalty.

"No. I think I'm gonna wait in the hall for a few minutes."

"Suit yourself, kid. I'm going in," and with that, he exhaled and walked through the door.

My grandmother had ended up in a place like this, sort of. I remembered a few visits to Rose Briar, the institution located in a neighboring town. In fact, Rose Briar was always a threat. "If you keep acting like this or that, we're taking you to Rose Briar!" Mom would bellow on the rare occasions when she wasn't getting her way. But my grandmother didn't know she was at Rose Briar. When the time came, she thought she was going to the hospital, and she loved to go to the hospital. She would have never gone otherwise. No 'spa' for her. The hospital was just fine. As the years passed, it didn't matter. She declined mentally and didn't know who any of us were anymore, much less where the fuck she was.

I wandered into the waiting area and found some weak coffee. I was standing by the window when my stepdad found me. He looked older than he had 15 minutes ago. Mother had a way of doing that to people. "Next," was all he said. I let out a breath I didn't know I was holding, tossed my paper cup into a waste basket, and walked off. How would this visit go? Would I ache, feeling all the blows and barbs, or would I fade out, steeling myself, disappearing in my mind? As I walked into her room, I heard, "Elia, what the hell have you done? You look just awful."

"Hi, Mom," I offered, absentmindedly tucking my hair behind my ear. "I just cut my hair, that's all."

"Well, it looks terrible. You always look ready for a funeral anyway, and now this. No one is ever going to want you if you keep doing stuff like that to yourself. But then, who has ever wanted you?" She laughed then, making me the butt of her jokes just as she always had. T wanted me, wanted to be my friend. I'd done a good job hiding my relationship with T. My stepdad never mentioned it and covered for me with little white lies to Mother when I needed him to. Ever since that one time I'd brought her over to my house, I'd learned to keep our friendship a secret. At least until Mom was taken away two years ago.

"How are you doing, Mom?" I tried to ask cheerfully.

She was across the room looking down at her bare feet planted on the yellow linoleum floor that mimicked the urine smell as a visual, her gown, hospital issue, her blond now silver streaked hair somewhat combed today, unpolished nails tapping together. She turned slowly and cut those evil blue eyes, our eyes, at me. "How do you think I'm doing, Elia? Do you even *care*?"

Uh oh. It was an off day. A bear day. My body instinctively recoiled. I'd grown to long for the Xanax days. The easier days. The days she seemed happy in her make-believe world. The days when she played the part of the beautiful princess, being taken care of by her staff, the center of attention. No. Today was not one of those days. Today was the type of day where she knew where she was. That this was no spa. She was pissed off. And it was all my fault. My stepdad and I had banished her and locked her away.

THEN

The best and worst day of my life happened when I was almost 16. In middle school, a few years before, I had begun cutting myself the day after I'd brought T over to my house for the first time when Mom was still around. Don't get me wrong. Having T in my life was the best thing that had ever happened to me, but I had to keep our friendship a secret. There was no way in hell I could let Mom know. There was no way Mother could stand my giving affection to anyone else. It would be a break of an allegiance. I was living a double life. I got those fleeting glimpses of happiness with Trudy and her family, and then, when I'd go home, I'd numb out, go through the motions, acting as my mom's whipping post, taking all the verbal abuse. It had only been verbal abuse up to that point. Late at night, in my room, that's when I'd do it. I didn't cut every day, just when I needed to feel something or nothing. Or I'd do it on the bear days.

I guess I was about 14 when T and I had wandered into *Mystic Blue* for the first time. It had been my idea. "Let's just look around," I'd said. T was wary, but she was in. Kelly waited on us that day. She was like a breath of fresh air, sage scented air. And I loved her immediately. She recommended a book to me, a book on solitary practice. At the time, I had no idea what that meant, but if Kelly suggested it, I was all for it.

I'd been keeping my friendship with T, my cutting, and my visits to *Blue* secret for a while. I'd been careful, really careful. My mom may have been into astrology, but witchcraft, oh Hell no. Mother thought that stuff was of the Devil, and no way would anything like that be allowed in her house.

The best and worst day of my life went something like this:

I'd come home a little after dark. I'd been over at T's doing homework. When I entered the house, there were only one or two lights on. It was mostly dark. And silent. I didn't think much of it at the time. I went up to my room, and that's when the shit hit the fan. There in my room, in the dark, like the boogie man waiting for me was Mother. She seemed calm, which should have been a red flag. "So…Elia…you're finally home," she said.

"Uh…yeah, I went to the library after school. I needed to do some research for a paper, Mom. Sorry…I lost track of time."

She was staring at me, glaring at me. "Oh, Elia," she said, rising up out of the dark, heading towards me. "You lie…so well." She was holding something in each hand. When she stepped into the light, she held them both out. In one, a book I'd gotten at *Blue* and in the other, my Exacto knife.

Oh fuck, I thought. I became very, very still. I didn't know what was going to happen, but never in a million years could I have predicted what actually went down.

"I'd been doing the laundry, Elia, and bent down to grab a sweater that was sticking out from under your bed and looky looky. How dare you bring this Satanic literature into my house! And what is this? Are you *still* doing this?" she said, waving the knife in front of my face. Her calm, calculating demeanor fading away, giving into rage.

Fuck, fuck, fuck, I thought.

"That's just my art knife, Mom. I use it at school for clay work."

"Bullshit," she said. "Just what the hell is this then?" She'd dropped the book now and was pointing repeatedly to the dried blood on the knife's edge. Crap. I hadn't cleaned it very well the last time. In fact, since I'd discovered *Blue,* I hadn't cut myself in a long time. I'd forgotten. I'd been careless.

"Mom...please," I said. "I, I, I don't know how that got there. Maybe...I just nicked myself accidentally the last time I used it." I was scrambling at this point.

"That's not what I think, Elia. Let me have a good look at you." She grabbed me, turned me this way and that, pushed up my sleeves. "Okay.

I have to do this. Elia, take off your pants," she commanded.

"Mom, *please*," I begged on the verge of tears.

"Do it!" She screamed. I unfastened the top of my jeans and slid them down. She began to inspect me. And there on my inner thighs were all the tiny scars I'd given myself over time. "Elia, I knew you must be up to something, but I had no idea what. Why are you still doing this? What? Were you looking for attention? Ha! Or what? Is this your way of dealing with your life, a *coping mechanism*? You have no fucking idea how hard *I* had it, living with your grandmother, and *I* survived. You are weak, Elia. And what of this book, Elia? The devil's work. This is not how I raised you. What do *you* think we should do about this?"

By this time, tears were streaming down my cheeks. Mom began to pace, making circles around me, tapping her palm with the Exacto knife. She was thinking, planning. Then, she stopped and looked me dead in the eye, her eyes, our eyes, boring into mine. "Well, I think there's only one thing we can do. Lie down on your bed, Elia."

I shut down, walking as if in a trance to my

bed and lay down. Some part of me knew that one day, one day something much worse had been coming. She stood above me, locking eyes with me, her eyes, our eyes.

"Now," She said, arms crossed over her chest, her steady manner returning, "You know how I feel about witchcraft, Elia. I won't have this in my house. And since you seem to like to cut yourself, maybe what you need is a letting."

My eyes widened. *What the fuck was a letting?* I thought.

"You see, Elia," she began, "You know what they used to do to people in league with the devil, like *witches*, hmm, Elia? Well, one way was to perform a bloodletting to purge the body of evil. And that, Elia, is just what we are going to do." And some strange, throaty laugh emerged from her.

Coming out of my haze, I pleaded, "Mom, no, no. Don't…do this. I promise I'll stop. I'll…get rid of the book. I'll… stop seeing T."

Mother stopped, knife in mid-air. "What?" She said curtly, "You are *still* seeing that girl? It's been years, Elia. You have *kept* this from me? You little bitch. How dare you lie to me! I am your

MOTHER! Your loyalty is here in this house! To ME!" And with that, she raised the knife and brought it down and across the top of my right thigh, slicing across muscle and sinew.

I screamed and cried out, "Mama!" calling out for the mother of my childhood. She lifted the knife again, and I squeezed my eyes shut. But the next strike didn't come. My stepdad had come in from work and grabbed Mom's arm. I opened my eyes then. He'd thrown her to the ground, lying on top of her.

"Elia!" he shouted, breathing hard. "Run. Call 911! Quickly. I've got her. GO!"

NOW

The day they took her away had been the worst and the best day of my life. The slice on my thigh had healed, left a scar. But I was still wounded. At least now, the visits were less. I'd just brace myself and get through this one. Then I could exhale, live a little and bide my time until my stepdad and I again felt the guilt, the twisted devotion, and we'd have to come back.

"Yes. I do care, Mom. That's why I asked," I said with phony sweetness, coming out of my brain fog. Mother just made her famous pursed lips and stared at me. Yes, I'd flinched at first, but I was less scared of her in here than I'd been at home. In here, there was nothing to break, no doors to slam, not a single thing to throw. One of the benefits of this floor of The Spa was that there was no way a patient could harm the staff or themselves. Well, except with her special version of verbal abuse.

"How am I *doing*, Elia? Well, let me tell you. I'm stuck here day after day, walking around in this 10 x 10-foot tiny room, alone with my own thoughts. I keep thinking about the terrible mother I had, all the things she did to me over the years, keeping me on such a short leash, rule after rule imposed on me, hurting me, and all of the other shitty things she did and then my thoughts turn to my husband and to you. And I pace this room and think about everything I ever did for the two of you, especially you, Elia. And for what? Ingrates! I wasted years of my life, sacrificing my own wants, my own needs to take care of you. And this is the thanks I get? Solitary confinement! I can't even write in this fucking place because I can't have pens or pencils or any fucking contact with the outside world!!!" She was getting louder and louder.

The room was sparse, but she was in a behavioral hospital after all, and there was a button by the side of the door. God, if I'd only had a buzzer like this at home. I could ring the bell now. And just like that, the staff arrived, and I could escape. "Goodbye, Mother. I'll come for another visit soon," I offered over my shoulder with another spoon full of sugar. All of that rant, her tirade, it was all bullshit. Sacrificed what? I was just an afterthought, someone in her way, keeping her from center stage.

As I walked away, I could hear her screams. I imagined the orderlies restraining her, her knocking the paper cup of meds from their hands, them having to pull out the big needle and knock her out. "You've lost your control over me, Mother," I smiled to myself. But…the smile quickly faded. I knew I'd regress, feeling the constraint, allowing myself to remain in the clutches of all the women who had come before me. But that was about to change. I was fucking sick of it. Tonight, I would discover just how to do this. Hopefully, I'd be rid of them all, and the ghosts of my girlhood would vanish.

CHAPTER 6

Tonight was the night. Well, not *the* night yet. I'd been getting excited since my stepdad and I had returned from The Spa. The ride back home had been quiet. This visit was over. It had been one of the explosive ones: All Hail the Bear. There were other kinds of visits, the ones when she was pretty well medicated and somewhat happy, in her own little world, the Queen Mother, taking callers and telling her subjects what to do and how to do it. Up and down and up and down, I just couldn't figure out why they didn't keep her medicated like that all of the time. It did make me wonder. Maybe the swings just weren't treatable with meds. Maybe it was all in her/my head. The links in the family chain clamped together so tightly. It was time for me to figure out how to get myself out of the chain. Tonight was the night!

I was meeting T in front of *Blue* a little past closing time. For the last two years since Mother had been sequestered, I pretty much did what I wanted, when I wanted. I was a good kid. My stepdad had known about T and my going to *Blue*. I never got in any trouble except for this summer school business, but that really wasn't trouble. Yeah, I was a good kid. I was beginning to believe it, too. Like I said, though, I think he was just hanging around since I was still a minor, but I would be 18 soon, and who knew what would happen then.

I saw T coming down the sidewalk. She was walking kind of slowly. Tonight, T looked like she'd stepped out of the movie *Grease* in a soft blue gingham full-skirted picnic-type dress, an ivory sweater tied around her shoulders and a sheer navy scarf holding back her hair. I went to meet her and even initiated a hug myself. I pulled back and took a look at her. She had a funny look on her face. Frankly, she was kind of green. "What's up, T?"

She exhaled, "I'm just getting nervous, I

guess, about seeing the Girls. Makes me have a queasy feeling in my stomach."

"No worries, T. I promise. Kelly wouldn't let anything negative happen. I just know it." And out of the blue, Kelly appeared in a floor-length sleeveless gauze dress, the color of an eggplant, and placed her hand on my shoulder, the one wrist bound with a huge stack of metal bracelets.

"Hey, y'all. New hairdos? The both of you? I like. T, you look sooo cute. And Elia, is that a *new* black shirt?" Kelly said. No, it wasn't new, but I appreciated Kelly's effort to lump me in with her compliment to T. My choices were simple. Not a whole lot of thought went into how I dressed. I did what I could with what I had, just throwing on something dark most days and dashing out the door. T and I looked at each other and back at Kelly and shrugged our shoulders in unison. Then she said, "Come on in. Join us." T looked at me sheepishly, and then we followed Kelly into the store. Locking the door behind us with a jingle jangle of her jewelry, Kelly then led us to the back for the Girls' full moon gathering. They were all back there, The Woo Woo Girls. Incense was burning, candles were lit, and some kind of Celtic music was softly playing in the background. And there they were, all of the Girls, seated in a circle around the table: Mary, Shirley, Ruby, also known as Bee Bee and Miss Constance. They melded together, the Girls, in their Belk's separates, sporting muted colors not unlike a scene of a painted desert at sunset with the occasional flash of burnt orange or teal. Their most distinguishing characteristics was their hair color, in Miss Clairol shades of Tawny, Light Ash, Copper #2, and Medium Brown.

"Wait, wait, wait. Just hold up there," Mary, the obvious leader, said, standing and holding her hands up in front of her as if to say, "Stand back." And T did, *literally*, take about three steps, backing into the shop. "Let's give Elia and T a good smudging before they enter the space. Sacred ground here, you know."

"Done and done," Kelly said as she lit the sage, gave it a blow, and made her way around and around me and T, waving the bundle in the air, making clouds of smoke ringing their way around us, supposedly clearing away any negative energy that had attached itself to us.

"Better do me twice, Kelly," I said jokingly, and she gave me a wink and an extra go-around before extinguishing the sage in a nearby bowl of salt.

"Shoes off, too," Mary added. "Now, you both may enter the room. Come. Join us." I went in first, and after I received loving hugs from Mary and the crew, T came in, and each of the Girls gave her quick squeezes, too. I could sense T relaxing. The air seemed electric, charged, the ladies all speaking at once, going on about summer pedicures and the like, welcoming us, asking us about how summer school was going. I wasn't sure how they knew we were in class this summer, but best not to question their skills.

"It's time," Miss Constance/Tawny said. Mary took her place near an altar at the front of the room. Bee Bee/Copper #2 stood opposite Mary, Miss Constance/Tawny, and Shirley/ Medium Brown took their places at opposite sides of the table. Kelly hung back near the door next to me and T. Mary opened the circle and called directions, each of the Girls raising their arms in turn as Mary gestured to the North, South, East, and West. I could see T, wide-eyed, taking it all in and her looking at me as if to say, "Yo. I thought we were just coming here to get information, not to participate in their *ritual*." I just took a deep breath and gave her a slow, small nod as if to say, "Be cool."

Shirley/Medium Brown spoke next, "I'll light the full moon fire."

What? I thought. *She's going to start a fire here, in Kelly's shop?* Kelly didn't move a muscle, so I stayed where I was, chilling. I craned my neck to see what would happen next. Shirley/Medium Brown approached the altar and lit a small fire in a tiny cauldron. There were other items there, too: incense, a few crystals of varying colors and sizes, and a cup of water.

Kelly, seeing me trying to figure out what was going on, leaned over and whispered, "The things on the altar represent the elements—fire, air, earth, and water. The items may vary at each ritual, but the elements are always represented." I again, nodded slowly. T caught this exchange, and I knew if I was cool, she would be cool.

"Now," Miss Constance/Tawny spoke again, "We will offer our intentions to the great mother by placing them in the fire along with any bay leaves indicating special prayers for others." One by one, the Girls made their way to the altar, either dropping in small slips of paper or bay into the flames. Kelly went forward last. (I would later find out that Kelly was an initiate, still learning and working towards being a full-fledged Woo Woo Girl.)

Once everyone was back in their spots, they began to sing, "May the circle be open and unbroken. May the peace of the Goddess be always in your hearts. Merry meet and merry part and merry meet again." They repeated this three times, then Bee Bee/Copper #2 went to the altar and took the cup of water and put out the fire.

Mary raised her arms above her head, clapping her hands loudly and proclaimed, "Aho, it is done. The circle is open! Let's eat!"

As the Girls began to set up tea and yummy things like fresh fruit, hummus and crackers, and lemon ice box pie, I was thinking to myself, *What? That was it?* The words were different, but the ceremony itself was not unlike the Sunday School classes and prayer circles my mother had dragged me to as a child. It was solemn, respectful, and orderly. Nothing like what I'd imagined.

"Penny for your thoughts, Elia?" Mary asked me as she gently guided me by the elbow out into the hall while the others began to eat and chit chat. T was watching, keeping her eyes on me.

"Well, it's just not what I thought it would be at all, your gathering."

"Things are not always what they seem, Elia," Mary continued, "What we, the Girls, practice is not unlike what you may experience at any other service or meeting. There is an order of events. Everyone has a part, everyone contributes. There is honor, reverence, and kindness. There is love. We pay homage to the great mother, The Goddess. It is a sacred circle."

"Gosh," I said, "I guess I've watched too many spooky movies. I mean, I just thought there would be more drama or trails of smoke or something...more cackling, maybe?"

Mary laughed at this. "Oh, Elia, witches are not necessarily what you've seen in movies or read about in books. The magic comes from a shared state of mind and setting intentions based on the combined energies of the group. It's amazing what you can manifest with the right power behind it. Now, you and your friend came here tonight to get some information, yes, about working your own ritual or spell?" I just shook my head yes. "Good,"

Mary said, "We'd *love* to help you."

We began to go back into the room when Mary stopped me, took both my hands in hers and looked me in the eyes. "I will tell you, though, Elia. There is such a thing as dark magic, energies you don't want to mess around with...forces...often malevolent. You and T must be mindful and careful. Any mistake may have negative consequences. Got it?" Again, I nodded yes, and as I did, I was thinking to myself, *Oh shit,* and just for a second, I thought I felt the hands of my ancestors reaching out for me, their ragged fingertips grazing my skin.

That night had been the full moon. I'd learned a lot. At the full moon, the Girls made offerings or intentions as well as any prayers or well wishes for friends or family members to the Goddess by placing the messages in the fire, sending the ashes and smoke out into the Universe. Their objectives or 'seeds' had been created on the previous new moon, and as the moon waxed, their desires grew, reaching fruition by the full moon. The waning moon, T and I discovered, was more about letting go or getting rid of things that no longer serve you. But heck, T and I had gathered that much from the book Kelly had loaned me. I was wondering if we were going to get any more information or help.

"It's really about your intention, honey," Bee Bee/Copper #2 had said, "What energy or thoughts you put behind your magic matters more than the day of the week or the phase of the moon. Keep it pure."

"Yes," Kelly added, "Keep it clear, simple. Y'all are just starting out, remember?" T and I nodded in unison, our eyes scanning the group. They were all nodding in unison, too.

That night, when T and I were walking home, we got to talking. "It was more fun than I thought it would be, Elia. And you were right. They all are kind of grandmotherly. Well, except Kelly, that is. She's like a kooky aunt." T giggled to herself.

"Yeah," I said, "I just thought maybe, I don't know, maybe there would be more drama. It reminded me of a ladies' luncheon, except for the fire and the chanting."

"Oh, Elia," T grabbed my hand and gave it a squeeze, "I know what you wanted. You wanted more *magic*. But maybe that's it, really. Just the group energy, the group dynamic, you know. That's probably all magic is, like *The Power of*

Positive Thinking. That kind of thing." T was raised in a super positive household, her parents were both counselors and maybe you bought into that stuff. I, on the other hand, was not. This was why I really needed this spell to work. I had to let shit go, and I'd tried everything else.

We were getting close to the crossroads now, where we'd split up and head to our homes. "Yeah, T, maybe you're right. But I still want to believe that there's more to it, more mystery. And, I know Bee Bee said it was really about the thoughts you put into what you were doing, but I still want to wait at least 24 hours when the moon is starting to wane."

"Ok. Alright. Fuck yeah. Let's do this shit!" T cried out. And she quickly covered her mouth and bent over, cracking herself up, trying to hold in her laughter, remembering we were in a residential area.

"Tomorrow night, your house?"

"Yes," T said, "My parents will be out at a work thing. The place will be ours. Until tomorrow night then," and with that, T lunged forward, waving her woo woo fingers in my face and then pulled me in for a big hug. All I could say was, "Yep. See you then." T turned and walked away, and I was left standing there, thinking of that one moment when Mary had held my hands in the hall. Yeah, I just knew there was more to this magic shit, this witchy stuff. She'd said there was darkness, and I knew well about living in the darkness, things lingering in the shadows, but I didn't have any idea at the time what could actually happen when I dipped my toes into spell work. I'd been standing on the shore with this woo woo for a while now, and it was time to put my feet in the water.

CHAPTER 7

I'd stayed clear of Mom's room since I'd collected what I needed for the work, for the spell. Her room had such bad energy, but hell, mine wasn't much better. For fuck's sake, that had been the room I'd been in when Mom had come at me with a knife, trying to cleanse me, the day it all went down. Then it was "Bye Bye Felicia" and "They're coming to take you away ho ho, hee hee, ha ha." Sometimes I think, "They're coming to take *me* away," but hopefully, with a little more work, I won't end up at The Spa too. Tonight, I'd get rid of Mother, even if it was only emotionally. Time to cut the ties.

Shit. I hadn't slept much at all last night. Nervous and excited, I'd tossed and turned, mind reeling up in my head too much. On the one hand,

I was thinking of how great it would be, how I'd have more peace in my life once T and I performed this spell. I'd be free from Mother. I'd be released, the clutch of all those who'd come before, The Horrifying Women, leaving me alone at last.

On the other hand, I kept thinking about Kelly and the Girls. The other night, it had all seemed so harmless and uplifting, even. Sure, we'd only attended one of their full moon ceremonies. Who knew what the other meetings were like?

I was trying to figure out how I was going to get through the day, pass the time until I could head over to Trudy's house when my phone vibrated. It was a text from T.

Hey. GTG somewhere with the rents today. The work thing they have 2nite, well it's 2day too, and they want me to come with to C their presentations and have lunch. I won't be gone all day, though. K? TTYL

K. CUL8R

Well, shit. Now, what was I going to do? I knew what I needed to do. I sighed and glanced towards the stairs. Grabbing a cup of coffee with one hand, I patted myself on the head with the other, saying "Good girl" to myself like I was praising a puppy. Then, I slowly headed up to Mom's room so I could make more headway in organizing and pitching her stuff.

Sitting on the floor, I looked around the room. I'd really made a good dent in this mess. I had boxed up her clothes from the dresser and the closet. Bins were overflowing with her journals and papers. I was thinking, *Man, I must be closer to being finished with this stuff than I'd remembered.* I remembered a lot of things....

THEN

It had only been a month or two since Mom had been taken away, ha, ha. The house seemed quiet, but there was definitely an energy, a heaviness present. In one sense, I could finally breathe easily, but in another, I still felt fear. This was about the time that the ghosts began to make their appearances. The first encounter I'd experienced had been in my bed that night. I'd rolled over in my sleep, and there she was, my grandmother. I'd know those eyes, her eyes, my eyes, anywhere, but her mouth, her mouth, was taut and … her lips…

they looked like they'd been sewn shut! She had raised one hand as if to reach out, then poof, she was gone, quickly dissipating and turning into a cloud of grey smoke, leaving only the faint scent of tobacco and rot—I would learn that each of The Horrifying Women had their own distinct odor. She was only there for a moment, in fact, it had been so fleeting, I hadn't even had time to mutter a sound, barely blink even. She'd scared the crap outta me, though—definitely a WTF moment. I'd kept my eyes shut tight the rest of the night. I didn't want to risk glimpsing another uninvited family member popping in from beyond the grave.

When I woke up the next day, I was even questioning myself, "Had I really seen what I thought I'd seen? Had it all been a dream?" Then, I headed into the bathroom. It was like a bad horror movie. You know, the predictable jump scare, only I hadn't predicted this. I got out of my hot shower; the mirror fogged up from the steam. I wiped my hand across the surface and thought I saw something. No, nothing in the reflection. No phantom was standing behind me. I looked behind the shower curtain. No, nothing there either. I exhaled, thinking the fear of my nighttime visitor had gotten the best of me. But when I turned around, there in the corner, huddled in a desiccated mass of mottled flesh and sinew, blackened eyes looked up at me from behind greasy strands of grey. I stood, frozen. *This* image did not fade as quickly as the one had the night before. Instead, it had lunged from its crouched position and grabbed hold of my ankles. I fell backward, kicking into the air as a scream escaped from my mouth. Then, it was gone, this one smelling of vanilla, pleasing and in total juxtaposition with how it had appeared! I looked down at my ankles, ringed with blackened soot like marks. They were marks, alright. I'd been marked that day. Mother had moved out, and the ghosts had moved in. The Horrifying Women were coming for me. The marks had faded in a day or so, but still. Later, when going through my mother's things, I would discover a box of old photos, faded and frayed. There, in the bathroom that morning, I'd run into my Aunt Laera, visiting from the beyond.

NOW

I'd gotten used to the ghosts over time, appearing in mirrors, skirting around corners, trying to make contact. But when I say, "gotten used to them," it didn't mean I was jumping for joy whenever they decided to make an appearance. Not feeling like doing much that day, I just lined up the boxes and bins, boxes of clothes to go to the thrift stores and bins of papers to go out with the recycling. The furniture, I guess we'd sell. Truthfully, I hadn't thought that far ahead. As I moved the last of the boxes near the door, I noticed they'd been blocking a small door in the corner. Was this another closet? Oh crap. Did I have more shit to sort? I made my way over to the tiny door, feeling a bit like Alice on her shroom trip, growing taller as the room grew smaller. I opened the door with a hefty tug. *How long had this been shut?* I thought. I peeked in and saw a small flight of stairs leading up. *Huh,* I thought. *Wasn't I already in the attic?* But here it was, another level. I backed up and closed the door, saving that for another day. I wasn't in the mood to run into any of my deceased relatives today. "Not today, Satan," I said, laughing to myself a little. "Maybe they will take me away, ha ha." I turned to head out of my mom's room, my eyes resting on the other door, Mom's closet. I squeezed my eyes shut, took a quick breath in, and darted out into the hall.

Suddenly, my phone buzzed in my pocket. What the hell time was it anyway? 3:40pm. *Oh shit*, I thought. I checked my notifications. T had texted 4 or 5 times.

The last one read,

Elia, where RU? I've been trying you for hours. I'm home now. Let's get this show on the road.

Geez. I must have been really lost in my head. I'd totally lost track of time. It was time to shower and head over to Trudy's. It was time for the spell work. I was ready to cut loose my family ties.

Sorry. Got caught up in cleaning up Mom's shit. B over soon. Cya.

And I meant just that. All you family spirits, see ya. Buh-bye. Let go of me and let the universe take you *all* away.

Before I left, I went to my own room to gather the things I'd need for tonight at T's. Mom's crafting scissors. Check. Her piece, "The Mother Who Never Loved Me." Insert eye roll. Check. I threw all of this into my messenger bag along with the book Kelly had loaned me, and what the hell, threw in a lighter and my sage, too. This was it. *The* night I'd been waiting for. The moon had begun to wane. It was the right time. Even though I was so close to working the spell, I still couldn't relax. I was passing a mirror in the hall and stopped to look at myself. My new do, sticking out in every direction. I had dark circles under my eyes, and my posture looked like that of an old lady, slumped over, head hanging. I quickly straightened up. At least I could fix that for now. What tha? Had something grazed my ankle? I thought I saw something move behind me. I snapped my head around to see some black shape seeping beneath a floorboard. Enough of this shit. It was time for the ghosts to get the hell out.

Just as I was about to make my way downstairs, something or someone made a quick dash, barely grazing me, leaving me cold. I broke out in goosebumps. Fuck. I was really, really going to be glad to get rid of my ancestors! Their hanging around my house was really starting to wear on me. This one was just a dark grey blob, probably one of my great, great grandmothers. It seemed the older the ghosts, the less definition the apparitions had, no form, just a blur, like a small, dark cloud.

Once outside, I picked up my pace. I knew T was waiting for me. I didn't know how the time had gotten away from me today. I had these gaps, chunks of time, minutes, sometimes hours, evaporating into thin air, missing. I just attributed it to my erratic sleep schedule. My sleep had never been good, but it had been much worse since my mom went to The Spa and the ghosts moved in. I was too anxious to sleep at night. The ghosts had never done anything too bad, or at least if they did something dreadful, it didn't happen often. I called it Ghost Shenanigans—lights flickering, the occasional piece of furniture shifting, outlets short-circuiting, finding random long gray hairs in the tub, and, oh, setting my hair dryer on fire that one time. The worst was when they made contact—poking me, pulling my hair, making temporary blackened marks or imprints on my skin, sometimes scraping me, leaving slight streaks of blood, my blood. I didn't think they could do anything lasting, though, to me anyway, the marks and scratches they made went away fairly quickly—they had no staying power. I wondered what it would take, what kind of energy they'd have to "borrow" to make a lasting impression? But shit, who wants to sleep knowing their house is haunted!?! They stole my sleep, my dreams. And ever since my stepdad had me cleaning out Mom's old attic room, I'd been passing out in there, on the floor, exhausted. *That* was one thing I was looking forward to—sleep. Sweet sleep and peace of mind.

I didn't even have to knock on Trudy's door. She was there, sitting on her front porch, waiting for me. She didn't say a word about me being late. And oh my, the look she had going on today! T had on a green wig, a hippy chick flowered dress with a belt, and a pair of sequined platform boots. Around her neck hung a giant rose quartz crystal pendant dangling from what was probably a hemp rope. And suspenders? Glitter? Bohemian glam?

I had to say something, "I get the getup T, but the wig? Are you channeling Kelly?" Actually, she looked like a cross between Kelly and Freddie Mercury. Or a mermaid on molly.

"I'm just trying something out," she said as she twisted the long, loose locks around her fingers. "I see you're dressed for the occasion too." T gave my skirt a playful yank. "Channeling your inner witch?"

"Oh, haha, T. You know this is just one of my well-loved thrifted numbers." Just another black dress from my collection of black dresses. This one ankle length with a drop waist. It almost hit the floor, the toes of my Docs peeking out from beneath a pool of inky polyester crepe. "And I did branch out tonight. I've got on a white tank under this. See?" And I ran my thumb beneath the spaghetti strap, pulling it out from my sleeve.

"I see. I see. Now, I've got something for you to see…."

I was wondering what T was up to when she just stood up, walked over to me, and gave me the hug I needed, the one I always needed. It was so unlike any attention I'd received growing up. I certainly never got any positive physical attention. And yeah, the ghosts made contact, but they really only ever scared the crap out of me. She pulled back, put her hands on my shoulders and looked me in the eye. "C'mon," she said, "Let's go get our woo on." Then, she turned around, and we headed, side by side, through her front door. At

the threshold, we paused, looked at one another,
not a word spoken and stepped through.

CHAPTER 8

When we got to T's room, the door was closed.
"Now, just a minute," T said, turning towards me.
"I've made some changes, preparations, really.
First, shoes off. We're about to walk into a sacred
space."

I looked down at my feet, chin lowered and
glanced up at T. "You're kidding, right?"

"Just do it," T pleaded. So, I gave in, eased
off my Docs. T took her boots off, too, bent down
and lined them up in the hall. Then, T slowly
opened the door.

I'd been in T's room hundreds of times, but
I was definitely not prepared for this. T's room
usually looked much like the rest of the house,
only with her own art hung up with pushpins,

and her photos were on a cloth-covered bulletin board affixed with lavender ribbons. The changes, though— *This* is what she had wanted me to see. I stood, mouth open, my eyes looking right, left, up and down. She'd turned her room into a smaller version of *Mystic Blue*. Tapestries hung from the walls and ceiling. There was a throw rug on the floor in the center of the room where a small table stood. Totally witchcore vibes, or hippycore, maybe? On the table were the items like the Girls had used in their full moon ritual, items representing the four elements. T had set up a candle, a crystal pyramid, a bowl of water and had some nag champa burning. My eyes rested on the candle. T, noticing this, said, "Yeah, I didn't think setting a fire in a tiny cauldron would fly with my mom."

I could not believe the transformation. "T! Holy shit! When did you do this?"

"Well . . ." T started, "The day you went to visit your mom in the insane asyl, uh, I mean the last time you went to see your mom at The Spa, I went over to *Blue* and Kelly was more than happy to help me out. I wanted things to be just right. Set the scene. Make sure things go off without a hitch."

This time, it was me, lunging at T and giving her a huge bear hug. "T, you're the best!"

She squeezed me back and said, "Now then, are you ready?" I held up my index finger, gesturing that I needed a minute. I removed my bag from my shoulder and put it down on the floor. I reached in and dug around, taking out the lighter and the sage, my mom's scissors, her papers, and finally, the book. I walked over to the makeshift altar T had set up. Careful not to disturb her handiwork, I placed the items just so and opened the book to the page with the spell. With Zippo and sage in hand, I faced T, nodded my head, and said, "Let's light this bitch."

And so, we began. After we'd properly smudged each other and the room, we put the sage out in the bowl of water (not ideal, but it worked). Then, we stood side by side at the table. I began to read aloud:

"*Take three (or the number of things you want to release plus one for yourself) strands of string or yarn, tie a knot in one end. Braid....*" and I stopped. "T, I forgot the string part! I didn't bring anything, string, twine, nothing."

"Don't worry, Elia. I remembered that part." That's T. She always had my back.

I read on:

"Braid them together. Pull one string out (this strand represents you) and cut this piece away from the other strands, while visualizing yourself walking away from the things you wish to sever from your life."

T handed me three pieces of red yarn. As I began to braid them together, I thought about what I wanted to let go of. First, my mom, of course. Then, grouping together the others, my ancestors — The Horrifying Women. I'd told T very little about the ghosts. I'd mentioned it once when they first started coming around, but T looked so freaked out that I hadn't said anything again until I'd decided to work this spell. I was trying not to freak her out too much. "I can't believe this is finally happening, T. I've wanted this for so long, and now it's really happening." T put one hand on my shoulder and gave me a gentle pat. One after the other, strand by strand, my hands shaking a little, I bound the strings together. I placed the cording on the table and exhaled. I hadn't realized I was holding my breath.

I began to read aloud again:

"*2. Make a list of items you'd like to release. Put pen to paper. Cut the paper into small pieces or strips. Burn all of the pieces. You may want to create a chant to repeat as the papers turn to ash.* Oh, you know what, T, I want to do this first, not make a list per se, but I want to use my mom's writing for this part, burn it."

T looked at me. "Elia, are you sure we should perform the steps out of order?"

"Yeah, it will be alright. Remember? Bee Bee said it's all about the intention I put behind the work. And I *intend* to cut my mom and the ghosts out of my life. Relax, we got this." T looked at me still, her eyes scanning my face. I knew she was looking at my dark circles. She knew I needed sleep, that I needed peace.

She sighed, "Okay, continue."

I took my mom's essay on her mom, my grandmother. All of us injured, all of us broken. I got ready to hold the paper to the lit candle and thought, "Oh, the chant." T just shrugged, her mouth jeering to the side. I began, "Sticks and stones may break my bones, but words will never hurt me." T let out a giggle. "Hey! It's all I could come up with on the fly. I'm not the writer in the family, you know?" Shit, I had to laugh too. As we laughed, the mood lightened, and I held the edge of the paper to the flame. We watched it burn and then submerged the bits that were left in the bowl of water. T quickly wiped one hand across the other as if to signify 'all done.'

"One part down," I said, "And one to go." I took the braid in my hand and carefully removed one piece of red yarn representing myself. My hands were shaking. This was it. This was big. I was getting rid of them once and for all, my mom, all of them. I began to work the single strand, back and forth between my thumb and index finger. With my other hand, I reached for my mom's crafting scissors. The shears shook in my hand. Under my breath, I muttered to myself, "Geeze, Elia, you want this. Get it together."

As I prepared to cut the yarn, T placed her hand on my shoulder again and started chanting, "Cut, cut, cut. Cut, cut, cut. Cut, cut, cut." I know she didn't mean to do it. I know she was trying to help me. But I was so focused on steading my hands she startled me, and I jerked back, tossing the scissors in the air. A cold gust of air seemed to come out of nowhere, forcing the scissors up, up, towards the tapestries T had so lovingly hung from the ceiling, trying to create a mood. Both of us frozen, agog, our eyes on the blades midair, catching the light from the candle. Then, down, down they came. We watched as they contacted my ankle, slicing through flesh, a deep gash spewing, spraying. I think I heard T scream. I began to bleed. I saw red, then black. Down, down I went. Another blast of air from God knows where extinguished the candle, and we were left in darkness.

THEN

It was the summer before I started high school. I'd been cutting myself on the sly for about a year, maybe a little more. I'd snuck in from T's house right before dark. My mom assumed I'd been volunteering at the library all summer, so I timed my daily return to coincide with the library's hours of operation. I walked past my Mom in the kitchen. We barely glanced at each other. Not a word was uttered between us. Mom had her head down, sullen, making dinner. She was wearing her sweats, hair all over the place. She was having an off day, a bear day. I could feel it.

I made it to my room and quietly closed

the door. With Mom making dinner, I knew I had some time on my hands. I was itching, needing release. That's what an addiction does. It calls you, won't leave you alone. You always want more. The cutting was my drug of choice. It's hard to explain, wanting to feel nothing and something at the same time. It had been a few days since the last time I'd done it. I was hungering for it. It wouldn't take long, just a quick one or two. One was good, but more was better. I had time, I thought.

I went to my closet, sat down, and reached inside my winter boots and felt around until I grasped my Exacto knife. I didn't even bother getting up. It was summer, and I was wearing shorts. Getting to my thigh right above my short's hem would be easy. I made one small cut and then another, side by side. I exhaled and closed my eyes for a second. Then, I looked down. There was a little blood, not much. I saw red. Then...I heard a scream. Oh fuck.

"Elia!" Mother yelled, "What the hell are you doing to yourself?"

Oh fuck. Oh fuck. Oh fuck. I sat there silent, totally busted.

"Elia, I came up to see if you could help me

with dinner, and I find you doing *this*, mutilating yourself!" Silence. "I, I don't even want to know how long you've been doing this," she said, swiping the knife from my hand, then she raised the hand holding my blade above her head and shook it as she spoke, "but as God as my witness, this is going to stop TODAY!"

"Mom, I..." I started but was quickly shut down as she grabbed me by the wrist. "Get up! Get up NOW and follow ME!" And 'the good girl' went.

Mom was taking me upstairs to her attic room. No good could come from this. This was her domain, well the whole house was really, but this, this was her chamber, All Hail the Queen. Once inside, she slammed the door. She grabbed my wrist again and pulled me over to her closet door. I didn't know what was behind this door. "Elia, I have no idea why you started doing this to yourself when I've given you everything a child could want. But this is going to STOP! Now, you are going to find out how *I* was raised, what *I* had to do on a regular basis, what your grandmother did to *me*. It's time to reflect and ask forgiveness." I'm thinking, okay, she wants me to pray, pray the cutting away??

Then, she opened the door and pushed me inside. I'd thought this was just her closet, but it was a little room. It was small, dark, cold, no carpet, nothing but what looked like a vanity with a mirror hanging above it. I looked around a little more to see stains and pellets on the floor, but that was the last thing I saw before she slammed the door, and I heard it lock.

"You stay in there, Elia! You stay in there all night! And you think, you pray. You think about what you owe me, and you damn well better be ready to apologize to me in the morning!"

That was the last thing I heard from her that night. Oh. I wasn't to pray to any god, ask any god for forgiveness. She was the god. Anything I'd done, I'd done to her. At that moment, I thought I felt a breeze. I was thinking, *where on earth was a breeze coming from in here*? Then, I felt something else. Something hairy, furry. Mice or rats, maybe? Tears filled my eyes, and I realized what the stains and pellets were on the floor. So here I would stay and think about what I'd done. I couldn't see anything. I could smell the stench of the urine, like ammonia.

Like Cinderella, myself, locked away, but there were no anthropomorphic creatures to entertain me, sing to me, help me—the rats couldn't say shit. Just me, sitting in the dark, in rodent piss and feces, every once in a while, feeling them crawling on me. I just sat there and cried, occasionally tracing the fresh cuts I'd made with my fingertips. It was soothing. Damn if the feeling didn't return, the call, the pull. Yeah, I would apologize to Mother in the morning, but I couldn't stop cutting, not then, anyway. I'd have to be much more careful next time.

NOW

I slowly opened my eyes, adjusting to the light. It was kind of difficult, but it wasn't because it was bright. I just felt so tired. The first thing I saw were the tapestries above me. Then, as I lowered my gaze, I met Kelly's hazel eyes, her brows furrowed in concern. Kelly to the rescue. She'd come in a hurry, obviously. I'd never seen her in a t-shirt and jeans. But Kelly's casual style still had an ease and grace about it. She smiled as she took a cool, damp washcloth and wiped my forehead. I was lying on T's bed, and when I looked to my left, there was T, right beside me, sitting as close as she could get, a mass of fake green hair next to her on the floor. T tried to smile, but I could see the fear in her eyes.

"How are you feeling, Elia?" Kelly asked.

I propped myself up on my elbows and looked around the room. I could tell it was still dark out. The tapestries were still hanging, and the table was still in the center of the room, but all of our ritual items were gone, including the braid and the scissors.

"I guess…I'm ok," I said. Then, I sat and swung my legs around, my feet trying to find the floor. While I was maneuvering myself, my ankle brushed the edge of the box springs. "Ouch!" I took in air between my teeth, and my hand reached for my foot. There, I found a bandage. My foot and ankle had been wrapped up, tended to. I looked at Kelly and T. The feigned smiles had left both of their faces. "Ok," I said quietly, "Would somebody tell me what the hell happened?"

Before either of them could speak, it all came back to me: taking off my boots, lighting the sage, burning my mom's writing, the braid, the scissors. Oh…the scissors…the wind. Where the fuck had the wind come from? And then, BAM, SLICE. RED. BLACK. I was sitting there, holding my ankle, shaking my head back and forth as though saying, "No, no, no." "All this waiting!" I shouted, "Waiting for the right time, the right moon cycle. Shit. Shit. Shit. And longer even. My. Whole. Life. I wanted, I needed to do this, perform this ritual, this spell, to get rid of my mom, the ghosts! And for what? Things to go south and blow it?" My eyes filled with tears. The dam was about to break.

Kelly spoke first, "Elia, when things went south as you say, T called me, frantic."

"I...I...I didn't know what to do, Elia," T interrupted, "You were bleeding! I was scared. I cleaned you up and bandaged up the cut. Then I called Kelly because I knew, I knew the spell was so important to you. I just didn't know what to do next. Kelly helped me move you to the bed, and we cleaned up. I've still got everything, don't worry." A couple of tears were now escaping down the sides of T's face as she tried to smile, to comfort me. And I knew, I knew T would still have everything. She always took care of me. I could depend on her and on Kelly.

"Yes," Kelly began, "Don't worry. Now,

then. Tell me more about the ghosts, Elia. You've mentioned them to me before, but I never knew if you were just calling your ancestors ghosts or if these women, your grandmother, your aunt, the line of women in your family, were *actually* ghosts."

"Well," I was a little hesitant, but hey, if I was going to talk about the visitations and appearances with anyone, it was Kelly. Now, it was time to let T in on everything, too. I took a long breath in, and then I let it out with a longer sigh. "It's like this." I went on and on about seeing these women, these spirits in my house, the way they appear, what they do, and the feeling I get whenever I leave the house or when I return and even the part about them touching me, grabbing me, and leaving marks. "The marks don't stay long. They fade after a day or so." T just sat there, mouth hanging open. Okay, I'd never told T anything except about how my grandmother and Aunt Laera had shown up the first time, and I'd sugar-coated that. Most of what I was saying right now was new information. Everything was out—the crazy was up on full volume. I'd laid all my cards on the table.

"I see," Kelly said. Now, *she* took a deep

breath in and let it out. She stood and began to pace around T's room. "Elia, I think, now, this is just a hypothesis, a guess, really. I think these things, these phantoms, may have attached themselves to you. At any rate, the items you brought from your home, there could be residual energies on them. I know you and T smudged yourselves and the space, but did you smudge everything else? T and I both silently shook our heads no. "I see," Kelly said again, "Well, I'll tell y'all what we're going to do. The moon is still waning. You don't have to wait another whole month. Tonight, get a good night's sleep, and tomorrow, you two get together. T check on Elia's cut, and the both of you make sure you have everything from tonight's ritual bagged up, and then after hours, come to *Blue*. I'll call the Girls, and we'll hook you up. We WILL get the ritual, the spell, right tomorrow night, okay? Bring everything from tonight with you. I'm going to head home now. I'm leaving you in good hands, Elia."

Okay. Everything was going to be okay. We were in this together, and we were going to get this right! And Kelly, man, she was the coolest. I don't know how I would wait until tomorrow night, though. I guess T and I could work on summer school assignments to pass the time. Then, my ankle began to throb, so yeah, that would be a distraction, too. As I absentmindedly rubbed the cut from the scissor's mishap, I noticed Kelly stop.

Before she walked out the door, she turned to us and said, "Oh, girls, by the way. I'd smudge again in here if I were you. That gust you described, that wasn't just the wind. That scissor snafu was no accident. There was someone here with you two, probably one of your kin, Elia. Well…goodnight then y'all."

CHAPTER 9

"Well, goodnight then, y'all." The last words Kelly had said before she left. Oh. And before that, *"Smudge again,"* she said, *"That was no accident,"* she said, *"Probably some of your kin Elia,"* she said. All I could think was, "What. The. Fuck." Yes, "What. The. Fuck" was what I was thinking in T's room the next day.

~*~

Last night, we'd watched Kelly go and didn't say a word for a long time. We went through the motions: lighting the sage, smudging the shit out of everything, bagging up what we'd need when we met with the Girls tomorrow night, taking down the tapestries etc., righting the room, returning it to T's *normal* bedroom.

I spoke first, "Well, I think that just about does it. Thanks again for calling Kelly and for bandaging up my ankle. Wanna meet tomorrow, here, and work on our last papers for world history?"

It was T's turn to WTF. "What. The. Fuck, Elia? Guess that's it…thanks…tra la la, back to summer school?? Are we going to talk about what went down here just hours ago??"

I swallowed my lips for a second and then drew in a deep breath and let it out through pursed lips. "T, I know all this woo woo stuff is new to you and yeah, I know you're not completely comfortable with it. And the ghost thing? I'm just used to it, I guess."

"Used to the ghost thing, you guess!?!" T shouted. Then, she remembered her parents might be home any time now and lowered her voice, "Elia," she said quietly, "I was so scared. And not just about what Kelly said. The ghost thing, Elia, you have never let me in on the extent of the ghost thing. I was scared, too, about all the stuff that happened before I called Kelly. You were bleeding a lot. And you know, with your history…" That was enough said. I knew what she was getting at.

We hadn't talked about it in a long time. I had to remember that she was just worried. Not judging, just worried.

"It's been a long while now, T, since I was cutting. I know it doesn't seem like I'm better, but truly, I am, really. The school counselors, getting to know Kelly, and, of course, our friendship — all of those things have helped me so much. I just," and I paused, sighed, "I just wanted to try to let go of this last crap once and for all, you know?" T slowly placed her hand on my shoulder so as not to startle me and nodded.

"I know," she said, "I know."

And that was all that was said last night. T walked me out. I made my way home. I was limping just a little. That mishap, those scissors had really cut the shit out of me. The closer I got to home, I felt the pull of the fingers, but it wasn't as strong. Maybe we'd accomplished something tonight after all. As I got ready for bed, my mind was reeling, playing over the events from the night. I was trying to go over everything in my head, see where it all went wrong. I was getting sleepy, though. As my head hit the pillow and I drew the covers up under my chin, my mind went to other thoughts. Had T been right? The cutting, any addiction, it's a slippery slope. That hunger is deep, to want to feel nothing and want to feel something. I'd have to be careful, watch for signs, triggers. I couldn't keep my eyes open any longer. I curled up into a ball, drawing my knees into my chest, my hand finding its way down to my ankle, and I drifted off, stroking the bandage like a pet.

~*~

Now, I was back in the present moment, back in Trudy's room, both of us hard at work. Nothing of the night before was mentioned. Everything felt back to normal. We were finishing up our second papers. For now, we worked, we waited. Time would pass slowly today, and then, tonight, we'd try it again, only this time, we'd have help. I know T was glad about that, and so was I. Kelly would help us. The Girls would guide us. And finally, I'd be free. For now, I continued to work side by side with my bestie. One hand furiously writing away, working on an outline for my last paper. The other hand, though, kept finding the bandage on my foot. And as time ticked by, I could feel my blood, my pulse at the site of the gash, beating in rhythm like a second hand of a clock, marking time, counting down.

T and I were both working on completing our summer school requirements. Three passing papers, and we'd officially be seniors. For the second paper, I chose the topic of the decline of the Vedic religions around the time of 600 BC. I was almost done and starting my outline for the third paper. The last paper was to be a comparative study of the two previous papers. This was just the distraction I needed to pass the time until tonight.

I had to put my thinking cap on for this one. Somehow, I had to tie Persephone to the Vedic philosophies, Greece, and India. What was I thinking? I planned on talking about the rise of Buddhism as well. That's one of the problems with overthinkers. Too much time and too much stuff rattling around in our heads. Ah, Persephone, she was my kindred spirit, that one. Well, in a lot of ways. I identified with the idea of the controlling mother, sure, but there was something more. There was that idea of the pomegranate. I imagined Persephone so alone, even with the ghosts in Hell around her. I'm sure she was lonely, lonely and starved. Eager to feel something and nothing. I could relate. When I close my eyes, I can see her taking a bite of that crimson orb, the flesh torn, raw meat exposed. Her finding a way to cope with her suffering. Hey! Suffering! I may be onto something here, tying Persephone's tale to the Buddhist beliefs about suffering.

I was so distracted I didn't realize what I was doing until T shouted at me. "Hey! Hey!" T shouted. "Look at what you're doing!"

Snapped out of my daydream, I looked around to see what T was talking about. Then I looked at her, and she pointed to my foot. Jesus. I'd just been pulling and pulling at the gauze until the cut was completely uncovered, and now, I was bleeding onto T's floor.

"Oh, shit, T! I'm so sorry. I wasn't thinking, or rather, I was thinking about something else. Sorry, sorry."

"It's okay. It's okay. I can clean up the floor. I was more concerned about you. Let's check you out."

T came closer, and I instinctively pulled away, wanting to hide, but then I remembered who I was dealing with. T breathed in and out a couple of times as she surveyed the damage. "It's not *too* bad," T said, "Let's clean it and get a fresh dressing. It's kind of deep, though. I wonder if you should have gotten some stitches."

"No!" I cried out and quickly lowered my voice, "No, no, T. It will be fine as long as I keep it clean, I'm sure." There was no way I was letting a doctor see this and getting into the whole "we were practicing witchcraft, and there was this ghost, you see . . ." Yeah, no. Then they would seriously be 'coming to take me away, haha.'

T helped me flush out the gash with peroxide and taped me up again. She was always putting me back together it seemed. Then, I wiped up the blood I'd dripped on T's bedroom floor. I packed up my bag, and T grabbed the bag of stuff from last night. That was it. We were ready. I was ready, ready to finish this, once and for all. There were no more words to say. T looked at me and gave my hand a squeeze. Then, she turned to leave her room. I was right behind her, but as I reached the doorway, it felt like the temperature dropped, like I was standing in a cold spot. I didn't feel any kind of gust like last night, but I was definitely cold, enough that I trembled. I began to rub my arms, trying to warm myself. I even found myself looking over my shoulder to see what, I don't know, a figure, a puff of smoke. But there was nothing. I shook my head, brushing it off and stepped into the hall. The cold left as quickly as it had come, and I felt warm again. I reached back, grabbed the knob, and closed the door.

CHAPTER 10

We found ourselves just where we were only days before. T and I stood outside *Mystic Blue*, just the two of us with our bag of stuff, waiting for Kelly to open the door. We both looked a little more subdued than usual. I had just thrown on a dark T-shirt with cropped cargo pants. And T was toned down for T—high waisted shorts, a boat neck t and, oh, well, a kicky black beret. I was thinking it must be nearing Bastille Day. The experience last night had changed us, aged us even, I thought. You just couldn't take this otherworldly stuff too lightly. We'd put more than our toes in last night. We were up to our waists now, wading through the witchy waters.

From behind the glass, Kelly smiled. She

seemed low-key, too, just wearing a long jade jersey maxi dress, kind of like a nightgown, chunks of turquoise resting on her collar bones, hair hanging down wrapped around her shoulders like a caplet. We'd all been through a stressful ordeal the night before, and we were all tired.

Kelly let us in, gave us both a hug, and said, "Okay, y'all. Let's go." We headed to the back of the shop. The Girls were already there: Mary, Shirley, Bee Bee, and Miss Constance. Now we knew the routine, shoes off, and a good smudging, then we'd be good to go. And I was good to go. I was ready. God, Goddess, whoever was listening, "Please," I said in my head, "Just please, let this work."

Besides the usual setup, there was a larger table in the center with space for our stuff. I felt myself shaking as I placed the items on the altar. The braid and my mom's scissors, was that it? I tried to think back to the night before. Before everything went haywire. I took a moment, thinking. Yes, yes, we'd completed part of the spell. We'd burned my mom's writing. We just had the ridding part to do. I guess I was taking a while, lost in thought because I jumped when Mary put her arm around my shoulders. "Oh!" I shouted, "You startled me, Mary."

"It's okay," she said, "It's all going to be okay. Now, before we begin, why don't you fill us in on what happened last night. Kelly gave me a brief run down when she called, but I want to hear it in your own words. Try not to leave anything out."

Mary and the rest of the Girls just stood there nodding, quietly holding space for me. How did I get so lucky to have all these great women in my life? All of them, Trudy, Kelly, the Girls. At that moment, I was counting myself very lucky indeed. When I finished, I took a deep breath and looked at T. "Did I forget anything?"

T just shook her head and said, "Nope." I had a feeling she'd be short on words tonight. I know this was not her thing, but damn, she was here for me like always.

"I see, I see," Mary said.

"It sounds like your intention was true," Bee Bee/Copper #2 added.

Shirley/Medium Brown, reminding me of T at that moment, only added, "Yep."

Then Miss Constance/Tawny spoke up,

"Yeah, sounds like that ghost of yours just fucked everything up."

Kelly laughed, and then the rest of us joined in. Shit, I needed that bit of levity. Mary took the lead at that point, "Well, whoever or whatever that was, they are not welcome here. Let's get started. And with that, she held out her hands to me and said, "Come. Join us."

Everything went about the same as it had during the full moon ceremony. Quarters were called, the sacred space was created. The only difference was instead of burning intentions, we'd work the spell. When the time came, all the Girls gathered around the table. Kelly stepped forward, too, and gave T a little nudge, and she followed suit. They all looked at me. It was time. I approached the altar and picked up the braid, the one strand representing myself still separate from the night before. I reached for my mom's shears. Shit, I was trembling again. Mary was quick to move closer to me and placed her hand over my hand to steady me. It was like I had my very own grandma witch. Together, we cut the single strand away from the others. Then, Mary spoke, "Since the elements are represented on the altar, we will burn the remaining strings, ensuring the separation." We all watched as the strings burned into nothingness. Mary spoke again, "The cords have been severed. Let's sing."

"May the circle be open and unbroken. May the peace of the Goddess be always in your hearts. Merry meet and merry part and merry meet again."

Mary raised her arms above her head, clapping her hands loudly and said, "Aho, it is done. The circle is open!"

Wow! I'd done it. We'd done it! I felt like a member, like I belonged to something big, like I was part of a family, like a full-fledged Woo Woo Girl.

Like a witch.

And with that thought, I felt a pulse. There were no cold spots here. Only warmth, an energy, a beat, the blood flowing through my veins. I stood there smiling, taking it all in, seeing the Girls chatting away, Kelly laughing at something Miss Constance/Tawny said, even T, grinning from ear to ear. I belonged. I still held the last strand in my hand, my fingers gripping it, holding on. The strand that represented *me*. My happiness, my future, was in my hands. I still felt a pulse as I put the last thread in my pocket. Then, my attention shifted to my cut, the gash at my ankle. The feeling was strongest at the site of the laceration. It was calling me. One fight was over, and another was beginning.

That night, I found myself at my house, alone. My stepdad was MIA these days. The house was empty. It was just me. Wait. Was it just me? It was just me. I didn't feel them. The invisible hands, the familiar tug as I neared the house. I was inside now, and nothing. It was gone. Wow. My shoulders relaxed. It really was just me. Reaching into my pocket, I pulled out the red yarn. My life was in my hands. Finally.

I started to make my way to my room and stopped in my tracks. What if it was just me? What if everything was up to me now? Yeah, my stepdad was around sometimes. Yeah, I had T and Kelly. I even had my tribe of grandma witches. I just stood there, standing in place, letting all of that sink in. I started walking again, passing the bathroom and into my bedroom.

Flopping down on the bed, I stared at the ceiling. I audibly exhaled. Holy shit! That was a lot to process. It was all exciting and scary at the same time. I got up and went over to my desk to put the red string away for safekeeping. As I opened the top side drawer, my gaze fell to the contents inside: post-its, thumbtacks, a couple of extra stylists, loose leaf paper. I set the red yarn on the desktop and took the papers out, and gave them a tap to straighten them out, and then I saw it. An Exacto knife. I laid the papers on the desk and picked up the knife. Honestly, I didn't think I had any more knives in my room. I could handle having this around now, right? I mean, I'd done the work. I'd let go of The Horrifying Women. I was free. Right? I didn't need this 'coping skill,' as the school counselors had called it. I held the knife in my hand. I closed my eyes and let myself remember, just for a minute, what it felt like. I remembered what it felt like to want to feel something and nothing all at once. I remembered well the feeling of relief, of control. And, of course, I remembered the feeling of shame of having a secret. I opened my eyes, put the knife back in the drawer and placed the papers on top of it. *There*, I thought as I shut the drawer tight, *Out of sight, out of mind*.

Lost in my reverie, I forgot all about the

red string. As I turned to kick off my shoes, my hand must have grazed the desktop, knocking it to the floor. But I didn't notice. I crawled into bed, stupidly thinking I had everything under control. Nestling in, I pulled the covers up to my chin and curled into a ball. *Yes*, I thought. *I have everything under control.* These were my last thoughts as I closed my eyes, drifting off as my hand made its way down to my ankle and just like a child with a blanket or a favorite stuffed animal, I fell asleep methodically rubbing the bandage, holding onto some fucked up sense of security.

CHAPTER 11

It just started to happen gradually, right after the night with Kelly and The Girls. T and I had turned in our second papers. One more, and we were good to go. Then, T's family had decided to take a summer vacation, and it really was just me. I was left alone. Alright, now I sounded as dramatic as Mother. Of course, I was not completely alone. I could call on Kelly if I needed her. And my stepdad, where the fuck had my stepdad been, by the way? He was around somewhere, I guess. So, I was not completely alone. Just lonely.

I had finally decided to look at my injury and assess the damage. I'd waited a couple of days until I knew it needed to be cleaned and redressed. I didn't want to risk an infection, but

I was also putting off looking at it. I knew myself
well enough. Honestly, I didn't know how healthy
I was at this point. I'd performed the ritual. I'd had
help. I did it, released it all. The ghosts seemed to
be gone. And yet, I was unsure about my mental
stability with T out of town.

In my bathroom, my now phantom-free
bathroom, I thought, *Okay, Elia. You can do this.
You got this*. I peeled back the bandage, wincing.
It was stuck good, all dried and crusty and oozing
a small amount of pus. "Crap," I said to myself.
Had I let it go too long? I hiked my foot up to the
sink and put my ankle under running water. The
scabby parts began to break away and run down
the drain. I was thinking, *How gross*. Then, once
it was all clear, I was face to face with the gash.
Shit, those shears had done a number on me. The
opening ran across the outside of my ankle and
ended close to my heel. I gingerly patted it with
a towel and traced the incision with my fingers.
I closed my eyes at that point. I began to bite my
bottom lip. I didn't have this. The desire was
strong, and I knew I was going to give in.

That's how it started, but it was gradual.
That night, I began to pick at the cut, hearing my

mom's voice from my childhood yelling at me, "Don't pick it! You'll make it bleed more!" But I kept on. The blood had never bothered me. The feeling of being suspended in time was a bigger payoff, a reward even. For a couple of nights, that's all I did. Pick. Pick. Pick. I'd redress it and wrap it up every time to conceal my handiwork, still making it to my summer school classes. Then, about five or six days past the ritual, I went to my desk and reclaimed my blade. Just a tiny slit. And there I was, at it again. I'd slipped. A few more nights passed, and the size of my cut, hell, let's be honest, the size of my mutilation had grown, now extending below my heel, making it challenging to walk without a limp, making it difficult to hide. I just told my summer schoolteacher as well as my stepdad (who made an appearance every once in a while) that I'd twisted my ankle, that I'd lost my footing walking along one of our town's quaint sidewalks.

Over a week had passed. I was lost, obsessing over my obsession. Losing track of time again, gaps here and there. T and her family were due back from their trip soon. They'd gone to the island, and the Wi-Fi there was always spotty. I had barely been able to contact her at all. How was I going to face her? I knew she'd be understanding. She was my T, my bestie. But I was embarrassed that I'd fallen back into this, this what, coping mechanism, addiction? And at that precise moment, there was a knock at the front door. I taped up my foot and ankle quickly. I'd gotten good at it, out of sight, out of mind. And as I hobbled down the stairs, I stopped. I could see the figure through the window in our front door. I gripped the railing and let out a long sigh. I felt like a rat in a trap.

It was Kelly, a vision in a snow white, almost translucent cotton dress. Her hair, more blue than green today, piled onto the top of her head, held in place with what looked like a gold braid. She was just standing at my door, waiting. She looked so beautiful, glowing even, exactly like a High Priestess—initiate no more. "Oh God, Goddess, whoever," I mentally pleaded. I sure as shit didn't want to disappoint Kelly. I slowly opened the door, head bowed, unable to make eye contact. I felt a gentle hand on my chin, lifting my head. I was greeted by a soft smile. All she had to say was, "Hi," and I fell into her arms, sobbing. She ushered me into the house, closing the door behind her.

We sat on the couch, side by side, and she let me cry it all out. After what seemed like an eternity, I caught my breath and told Kelly everything that had happened since the night at *Blue*. She sat very still, nodding, taking it all in. Then, when she could get a word in, she said, "Elia, take me up to your room."

THEN

The summer before my freshman year, the time I got caught by Mother, and she locked me away with the rats, was when I'd started popping into *Blue* on a regular basis after school. At first, I went without T. I knew it would freak her out, the crystals, the candles, the occult books. I'd wander around the store, looking at jewelry, every now and again picking up a book and leafing through it. After a couple of weeks of this, Kelly introduced herself and asked me if I needed any help. I didn't fall into her arms sobbing that time. Shit, I'd just met her and was trying really hard to not fall completely apart. *Did I need help?* I thought to myself. No, I still didn't go to pieces, but my eyes filled with tears, and I couldn't speak. I just stood there staring down at my feet. After a few seconds,

I composed myself, took a deep breath and said, "Yes. I do need help." Kelly took me aside, made me a cup of tea, and I spilled my guts, all of it, wacko Mother, my cutting obsession, all of it came out, as they say, "warts and all."

To this day, I don't know how that happened, how I was so quickly able to confide in Kelly. Chalk it up to the right time, right place, or just intuition. Or just maybe the night I'd been locked away in the dark with the rat piss was the wake-up call I needed. I was desperate to have a woman in my life that cared. Sure, I had T, but I craved the attention of a kind woman, a mother. Kelly wasn't technically old enough to be my mother, but she was what the universe gave me. My soul ached, and I was hungry. The local green haired mystic fit the bill.

My life changed that day. It didn't happen overnight. I kept going to see Kelly and eventually introduced T to her, too. Kelly convinced me to come clean to T and to get with a school counselor and work some stuff out. T was totally and completely okay with it all. I don't know why I hadn't told her about my cutting before. Shame? Guilt? That's all part of dealing with addiction. It was going to be work, but I just had to take it day by day. And I did. Or I had. Now, it felt like I'd have to start all over again.

NOW

I took Kelly to my room, and we sat down on the bed. Then, she turned to me and said, "Elia, where is it?" I knew what she meant. She wanted to know where my knife was. I was too tired to fight it anymore. I didn't hold back. I just got up and walked right over to the desk, trying not to put weight on my foot. But before I opened the drawer, I stopped and looked down. "What is it?" Kelly asked, craning her neck, trying to see what I was looking at. I bent down and picked up the red string, the thread that had represented me from the ritual.

"Huh," I said, "I'd forgotten all about this."

Kelly knew what it was. "Yes, Elia. Yes, you did. You forgot all about yourself."

I clutched the string to my chest and looked up at the ceiling, and then I closed my eyes and exhaled. I *had* forgotten about myself. I'd done some good work, and then, left to my own devices, I'd fallen back into the old habit. We went back and sat on the edge of my bed, me working that red string between my fingers. "Shit. Shit. Shit," I said, slowly shaking my head from side to side.

"Elia, this, the cutting relapse, is not your fault. I'm sure you were triggered just by the idea of it being part of the spell. Also, I think something else may have happened, too. Remember when you and T tried to work the spell on your own? Remember burning your Mom's writing?" I nodded, not sure where Kelly was going with this. "Do you remember anything else specific to that part of the ritual?"

I had to think. It had been a minute. I began to picture it in my mind. "I can't think of anything, Kelly," I replied.

"Think back to when you were gathering all of the things you needed to perform the spell, Elia. Think." And that's when I remembered. When I had first got all of that stuff out of my mom's room, I'd cut myself on accident.

"Oh wait, I do remember something. I had cut myself when I first grabbed my mom's shears. Some of my blood got on the paper." Kelly put her head down, her hands folded in her lap.

"Elia, I think that is a big part of it, the relapse.

You see, all of the light, all of the love and good intention, still . . . there is a darkness." I was silently shaking my head, yes, very slowly this time. "Elia, whenever you include blood in any kind of spell work, the blood intensifies the results. Somehow, I think you inadvertently inserted yourself into the ritual, not just the letting go and separating yourself from the women in your family with the braid work. You were literally cutting yourself out, energies got crossed, and the intention was muddied. You have to be incredibly careful, Elia. Remember that."

"Kelly, I know what I need to do. It's just hard, that's all. SO hard. It's just that, that, you know when you don't fit in...when your family is so different from everyone else's... when you've always been Other..." Kelly stopped me there, stood up, and took me by the hand.

She dragged me into the bathroom, and we stood side by side, facing the mirror. All of a sudden, the floor became really interesting. "Uh uh," Kelly said, "Take a good look in the mirror." I glanced at my reflection: my tear-streaked face, my black hair/blond roots looking kind of like a skunk, pieces sticking out in every direction, and

I couldn't remember the last time I'd changed my clothes. "I see a fucking mess is what I see."

"Uh uh," Kelly said again, "No negative self-talk. I see a mess, too. Truly, it's not one of your better days, Elia." I had to laugh at this a little. "But I see a *beautiful* mess, Elia. We are all of us broken in some way. Take it from me. Being different or Other, as you say, is okay. In fact, it's fucking a-mazing!"

I'd never heard Kelly say the F word, and I had to laugh some more. It felt good. "Ok," Kelly started, "I know you think it will be hard, and I'm not saying it won't, but you've done it before, and you can do it again! Just take baby steps. It's like the practice. There are steps, guidelines, processes. I know you wish the woo woo witchy stuff was more exciting. Maybe when you started connecting with the Girls, you thought there would be, I don't know, robes, smoke, chanting in Latin, but like Bee Bee said when you were with us the first night, it's about intention. And that's the real magic, Elia, committing to something and seeing it through. That's how you live an enchanted life and can see your dreams become reality. And having support helps. So, tomorrow morning, you're going to call your old counselor and make an appointment. Then, you are going to tell T. Y'all have been friends for a long time now, and she deserves to know. Don't shut her out. Are you home alone tonight?" I nodded yes. "Okay, then I'm staying over. The very first thing we are going to do is get you cleaned up. Maybe start with clean clothes?" Kelly now grabbed her nose, indicating that I smelled. I took a whiff under one arm. Whoa. Shit. Yeah, I needed a shower. We were both chuckling now. And I had happy tears running down my face. God, Goddess, I needed this release! "Oh, and after that, we're going to address the elephant in the room."

"Huh?" I said, my eyes darting from left to right.

"Well," Kelly continued, tapping her fingers together, "It's not *really* an elephant. Now, I'm not saying the spell didn't work. I don't feel any spirits or ghosts hanging around. Well…maybe just one. I felt it when we came in here, in the bathroom. Didn't you once tell me this is where you've seen your Aunt Laera? There must be a reason she's still here. I can sense it. Some unfinished business, maybe. Yeah, I don't think she's going anywhere, not without a fight anyway." With a twirl of her White Witch Stevie Nick-ish skirts, her blue bun bobbing, Kelly was out the door. I was left standing, my jaw dropped in shock.

And all I said to myself was, "Well Fuck."

CHAPTER 12

The next morning, Kelly and I set to work on performing a clearing. I didn't really have what Kelly needed on hand, so we just ended up doing a quick and dirty circle of sorts, swept the house from back to front and smudged the shit out of everything. We didn't know yet if it had worked. If it hadn't, Aunt Laera would have to wait for now. Granted, I wasn't as sensitive as Kelly, but I didn't *feel* anything now. Maybe that was a good thing?

Kelly hugged me goodbye and left to open the shop. The next thing I did was call my counselor. I reluctantly told her what was going on and then scheduled an appointment for that afternoon. Normally, it took over a week to get in with her, but she and I both agreed this was an emergency of sorts. That afternoon would be the beginning of months of sessions. And I knew I had to stick with it. Now, it would be time to contact T.

Trudy and her folks had gone to the island for their summer vacation. With the lack of coverage on the island, our texts were short, scarce.

Hey T? How's ur vacay?

Gud. Hot. And boring.

Miss u.

Miss u2. Everything k?

Yee. Fine. Everything's fine.

LOL. Gud. L8tr.

That was it. For over a week, that had been the extent of our communication. How could I tell her over text that everything was *not* fine? I didn't want to bug her or ruin her time away. I knew I had to tell her as soon as she got back.

It was time to come clean. I couldn't blame anyone. No one had abandoned me. Sure, life with

Mother had been a ride on the crazy train, but the people in my life now, they were solid. I had to take a long, hard look at myself and take responsibility. It was almost my 18th birthday. In the eyes of the law, I was an adult, and I needed to start acting my age. I'd had a lapse, reverted to a bad habit. Wait. No negative self-talk, Kelly had said. Addiction comes in many forms, and I used this one as a way to manage things. I just had to rely on other tools. I had to be gentle with myself, practice self-care and love myself, all that crap. I only had one more year of high school, and then, hopefully, I'd be off to college. Now was the time to get my shit together.

The next day, T and her folks got back from their trip. I told her I wanted to meet down by the bay and hang. This time of year, the weather was dismal, the heat, suffocating. Any kind of hair or makeup attempt was futile. You just melted. When I saw T, I could tell we'd both chosen function over fashion-just loose t-shirts, shorts, and flip-flops in these dog days of summer. T was rosy cheeked, fresh freckles dotted her nose and forehead. Her hair was strawberry blond from the sun. She was wearing a sky-blue Beach Bums shirt from the bakery on the island, also known as BB's. We met at our favorite spot. Under the oaks, a welcome breeze off the water revived us as we sat together on a bench, side by side. T had a Beach Bums t-shirt for me too, black, of course, as well as a puka shell necklace. She was always trying to accessorize me. She started to tell me about her trip, but I interrupted her. I didn't fall to pieces like I had with Kelly. I was mostly cried out. Well, almost. I told her everything, everything that had happened since she left, my voice catching here and there.

At first, she didn't say anything, and I was thinking, *Oh, fuck. That's it. The last straw. I'd finally pushed her away with all of my bullshit.* I was staring at my hands in my lap when I heard a sniff. And then another. I looked up, and T was crying. Now, I really felt like shit. But before I could say anything else, she looked up at me with those grey green eyes, greener outside, grabbed me fiercely and held me tight—a famous T hug. We stayed like that for a long time. And that was it. No more words were spoken.

T looked in her bag for tissues. I gracefully wiped my snot on my sleeve. This broke the silence, and we laughed softly. Why did I think T would react to my news any other way? I had to start believing in people. I had to trust. I didn't know how to do this. But my God, my Goddess, the women in my life *now* were something! It would take time, like anything else. But I'd reached out. I had support. I had hope.

~*~

It was the end of July. The air in our coastal town was heavy, thick. Everyone was moving slowly like they were weighed down. There was a run on sweet tea, and the lines at Frank's Pizza and Ice Cream Shack seemed never ending. I couldn't figure out how they never ran out of ice cream there! In about a week, T and I would turn in our last papers, and that would be that. Summer school done. Booyah! We'd still have a few weeks of fun and R and R before school started back up. And soon, it would be my birthday. It was the season of Leo, and I was turning 18.

After I'd had my 'talk to's' with Kelly and T, things began to look up. I'm not saying it was easy. I was still fighting the urge to give in to the craving. There were days I was downright hungry for it. My old school counselor had referred me to a therapist in town. She was an MD. After I turned 18, I could get my own prescriptions from her, in

WOUNDED   149

case. I was waiting on that, the in case. I didn't really want to rely on meds. I'd grown up seeing my mom on pills and not on pills, altering her moods. So, I was waiting. I'd said before I never knew what version of my mom I was going to get, and that was no fucking fun. I wasn't ready to be a Dr. Jekyll Mr. Hyde myself, much less foist those foreign forms of me on my circle of support.

Before I knew it, it was my birthday! I was actually looking forward to it this year. Hell, I got three celebrations this year. There's the rule of three. Lots of things come in threes. Good things come in threes. Better times had to be ahead. The night before my birthday, Trudy's family had me over for dinner. T's mom made my favorite: burgers and crinkle fries. The meat cooked just the way I liked, pink with just a little bit of blood, juicy. T's parents were playing Classic Rock, spinning vinyl. They even let me and T have tiny glasses of champagne! And T and her parents gave me a present. More jewelry and a sundress the color of a ripe peach. Okay. I was getting the hint. Maybe it was time for me to come out of mourning and pay attention to how I looked more. That's part of self-care, too, right?

The next day was my actual birthday. T and I spent the day together. We went out for breakfast and spent most of the day walking around downtown. We had to stop every once in a while. My 'injury' was still bothering me, but it was getting better. I limped a little. After picking up a couple of coffees from BB's sister shop, we headed over to *Blue*. Kelly greeted us as we came in. Her hair was a striking blue today, somewhat like a Smurf, but it was cool. Kelly could pull it off. And I think I caught sight of fresh ink on the inside of Kelly's left forearm. Looked like some kind of sacred geometry or symbol. I'd have to ask her about that later. She and T locked eyes, hazel to grey, and the next thing I knew, they were both taking me by the hand and leading me to the back of the shop. All the Girls were there—Mary, Shirley, Bee Bee, and Miss Constance. They all shouted, "Surprise!' and then wiggled their fingers in the air. I think a couple of them may have also said, "Wooooo," in sing-song voices. They had set up the back room just for me. There was coffee punch, pimento cheese sandwiches with the crusts cut off, and chocolate cake.

"We got you, didn't we?" T said.

"Oh yeah. Y'all sure as hell did!" I shot back.

Kelly came up then and gave me a hard squeeze, and said, "Happy trip around the sun, special girl. Or should I say woman now? I can't believe you're 18!"

"That's right," Mary added. "Elia, now that you are 18, we'd all like to officially welcome you into our moon circle. Soon, we'll have a ceremony, but today, we'll just cut loose and cackle our heads off!"

"Trudy will be welcome too when she comes of age if she's interested," Shirley/Medium Brown added.

"Yes, yes," Bee Bee/Copper #2 said, "They get it, they get it."

Miss Constance/Tawny broke in at that moment, "Okay, enough of all that, formality and ritual later. Let's eat, drink and be merry. Aho aho, let's go!"

We spent a couple of hours doing just that: eating, drinking, and making merry. Kelly brought out instruments, and we jammed, sort of. It was comical. Bee Bee/Copper #2 read cards. T seemed more and more relaxed around these gals. And there were gifts! Kelly gave me a few really nice quartz points and a piece of black tourmaline. The Girls gave me a beautiful blank grimoire. I had the best time! So much laughter. So much love. These women, my women, loved me. I had found a tribe. I was home.

Kelly smudged all of the new treasures. I hugged everyone goodbye and thanked them for the lovely gifts. Then T and I started to walk home. "Wow, I have had the best birthday, T! I know you had a hand in both of my celebrations. Your parents are so awesome. The party with Kelly and the Girls was a-mazing! And I know I have you to thank for getting it all together."

"Hey," T said, "It wasn't all me. Elia, don't you get it? My parents, Kelly, the Girls — ALL love you. They all care. We all got your back." I grabbed a hold of T and held her tight. We stayed that way for a couple of minutes right there at the crossroads, halfway from her house to mine.

Finally, we let go and said bye for now. There was still plenty of daylight this time of the year. As I got closer to my house, I didn't feel that oh so familiar grasp. The ghosts seemed to be gone. Maybe Aunt Laera too? I wasn't sure. Hopefully, the last clearing Kelly and I had performed had done the job. Before I had too long to think about that, I noticed my stepdad's car was in the driveway. I couldn't remember the last time I'd seen him come to think of it. I picked up my pace. Hell, I was in such a good mood, I was looking forward to seeing him.

"Hello?" I called out.

"Hey there, Elia," he said from the kitchen, "Come on in here."

I walked into the kitchen, and there on the table was a birthday cake, 18 candles blazing. "Happy birthday, Elia. Make a wish. Blow out the candles." I was taken off guard for a moment. Sure, I'd had birthdays before in this house, but I never would have thought he'd have come up with this on his own. I took a deep breath in, and then, with a whoosh, I exhaled. Shit. Two or three left. I blew again, and then they were all out.

"Guess I don't get my wish, huh?" I said, shrugging. He just made that tight grin that looked like a straight line running across his face.

"Go ahead. Sit down, Elia. I'll cut you a piece. Then we need to talk." My stepdad put a huge piece of cake in front of me and poured a glass of milk, and sat down across from me. "Elia," he started,

"I know it's never been easy. Hell, it wasn't easy for either of us living with your Mother." I took a bite of cake and just nodded in agreement. "And I don't want you to think I don't care about you, but . . .." It was then he slid a large envelope over to me. I hadn't even seen it on the table. I'd been so surprised by the cake and stuff.

"What is this?" I asked. He didn't say anything, so I went ahead and opened it. I didn't really know what I was looking at.

"It's the deed to this house, Elia. You're 18 now, and I thought it should go to you. Like I said, honey, it's not like I don't care. I just, I just can't stay here anymore. It's been long enough. I've served my time. I know it's been no picnic for you, either. But you're 18 now. Your Mom is gone, and this house should go to you. Now, I understand if it's too much, and we can talk about selling it and moving you somewhere new, somewhere you can start over. *I* just can't do this anymore." I sat there, speechless. He went on, "I haven't been around much lately. One, I was moving my stuff out little by little and two, I wanted to see how you'd manage on your own. Elia, I think you've got this, kid. You've always been very capable, adaptable. You had to be. I've moved out now, not too far away. And I'm not cutting you off. I've set up accounts for you to help you out with living expenses. I'm covering your health insurance through college. The house is paid off. If you need anything, all you have to do is call, Elia." Silence. "Elia, please, say something."

I was in shock; I mean, for real. "It's... okay," I managed, "I know it hasn't been easy for you. I understand...I do." It was understandable. Weak on his part but understandable. He seemed relieved.

"Good. Good," he said, seemingly satisfied, "Oh, there's a set of keys in the envelope too, and all of the rest of the keys to the house, to closets, drawers, they're all in that junk drawer near the fridge. Oh...and today...I got all of the stuff you boxed up out of your Mom's old room. It's empty now. Elia, I'm going to head out soon. Are you going to be okay?"

"Yeah," I said softly, then I corrected myself, shaking my head, "No, I mean...yeah, I'm fine. It's all fine. Everything's fine. We both deserve a little happiness, right?"

"That's a good girl," he said. He came

around the back of my chair and put his hands on my shoulders, and said, "Just call me if you need anything. I'm happy to help. Oh, and happy birthday, kid. You are right. We *both* deserve a little happiness." And then, he left. And I was left sitting there with my mouth full and a fork in my hand. I'd had three birthday celebrations. Good things happen in threes…but was this a good thing?

It took me a while to leave the table. I just sat there thinking, trying to make sense of everything. On the one hand, I was alone and starting over, trying to handle finishing school and getting to my therapist, and now I'd have to worry about the house and bills, but maybe not so much. My stepdad said he would help, right? I pushed my chair back from the table and started up the stairs. I was standing in the hall outside of Mother's attic room with my hand on the doorknob. I took a deep breath and went in.

I flipped the light switch. It was empty. Everything was gone. I walked around. No cold spots. It didn't feel like any of the old ghosts, The Horrifying Women, were hanging around. I was alone. I saw the door to the closet where Mother had shut me in that one night. I was *not* ready to go in there. Then, I noticed the other small door. I checked the knob, twisting it side to side, right, left, right, left. Locked. Shit. Huh. Maybe the key was in the junk drawer. Maybe I'd look for the key and explore that floor in the light of day. Not tonight, though. Yes, on the one hand, I was alone. On another, I was free. Well…almost. There was one more thing I needed to do, one more thing I needed to release. It was time to move on, but first, I needed to face the last living, horrifying woman.

CHAPTER 13

The next day, I decided to take the bus to The Spa. I'd use the ride over to clear my head and think about what I actually wanted to accomplish on the visit. I knew there was no reasoning with her. I'd had enough counseling sessions and read enough books to know she'd never change. This visit was for me. Call it the last rite, out with the old. I was letting go for good. It was time. I was pretty certain this would be the last time I would see Mother. This was the closure I needed.

It was just me this time, no Stepdad. Shit, last night had been weird. I had my own house now, all to myself. Pretty freaky. I had no one to buffer this visitation. The ride over helped me screw up the courage to face Mother. And if that wasn't enough, I'd put the black tourmaline that Kelly gave me in my pocket for protection. At the last minute, I decided to put on some lipstick, painting myself for war.

After entering The Spa, I practiced walking normally. I tried to put as much weight as I could on my good foot and adjusted my balance. The gash wasn't completely healed, and I had trouble putting my full weight on it. Then, I found myself standing outside the door to her room. There was nothing left to do but go in.

I entered, the door closing behind me. Mother was standing on the far side of the room with her back to me. "Well, hello, Elia," she said without turning around. "To what do I owe to this visit today? What, you couldn't make it over here on the actual anniversary of the day I gave birth to you? Oh," then she was moving slowly, turning around, "Happy birthday, Elia," but there was nothing *happy* about the way she said it. I noticed that her hair was a tangled mess. It was a bear day.

I wasn't giving in to my fear. "Thanks, Mom," I answered matter-of-factly, even though I felt the sting of her referring to *my* birthday as *her* accomplishment. No reaction on her part. She steeled herself, standing there in her thin hospital gown, feet bare, wild hair, staring me down with those evil blue eyes, her eyes, my eyes. I didn't budge, though. Oh…it was on.

She moved first, taking a step towards me. Shit. I jumped and stumbled. And when I did, I lost my balance, my weight shifting to my hurt foot. My legs went out from under me, and I crumbled to the floor. I looked up at her sheepishly and, using my hands for support, helped myself up to standing. Then, I took a few steps towards her, my limp now obvious. I stood straight and tall, squared my shoulders and looked right at her, daring her to say something.

She started to laugh. She doubled over and kept laughing like a deranged person. Seriously, I didn't know when the hell she was going to stop! It was unnerving. Finally, she was quiet, took a deep breath, and before I knew what was happening, she got this demented look on her face and ran, heading right for me. Without a word, she threw herself into me, tackling me, forcing me down to the hard yellow linoleum floor. We landed with a *thwack*, the side of my head crashing into the garbage can on the way down. For a second or two, I saw stars. The next thing I knew, she was on top of me, pinning me down. The sight of me limping had stirred her up. As we scuffled, neither of us made any audible sounds, just grunts and huffs under our breath so as not to be heard by staff. I struggled, and she fought me. Damn, she was strong for someone who was locked up in a 10 x 10 room most of the time. Mother got a hold of my ankle and pulled up my pants leg. Off came my shoe and sock, and then, she started with the maniacal laughing again. "Oh, Elia," she said breathlessly, "What have you done to yourself now?" Shit, this was it. No turning back.

Mother began to remove my bandage, more like yanked it off quick as she could. She stopped for just a moment, turning my foot this way and that, causing me to wince and bite my lower lip. Then she paused. She began to speak again, this time her tone cool and calculating, "Elia, what *is* this obsession you have with trying to draw all the attention to yourself? You think *you* belong in the spotlight?" She stopped again, looking up at the ceiling and shaking her head. Then she closed her eyes. When she looked at me, a strange toothy grin spread across her face. "My God, Elia. You're just like your Aunt Laera."

THEN

My mom was 8 years old when her big sister, my Aunt Laera, left home. At 18, she was ten years mom's senior and had, until that point, tried to protect my mom the best that she could from their mother. My grandmother was not just your regular control freak. She was batshit crazy. Her self-adulation was coupled with what the Germans refer to as schadenfreude, taking great pleasure in the pain and misfortune of others. My grandmother was diabolical. My own Mother's mad laughter and conniving tones had nothing on her. And when my Aunt Laera moved out, my mother had no one to shield her from my grandmother's wrath.

This type of mother, like my grandmother, often favors one child over another, making one the golden child and the other the scapegoat. Even at 8 years old, my mother had tried to do everything right, tried to please her mother, but she could never measure up to Aunt Laera's star quality. Laera could do no wrong in my grandmother's eyes. When Aunt Laera went away, things only got worse for my mother. You think my mother came up with the intimidation tactics, the degrading chatter, the disproportionate punishments, the banishing and locking away on her own? Oh, hell no. She'd had a great teacher. Mother had learned to hate, was filled to the brim with anger, my God, my Goddess, the anger. My grandmother had made her suffer, made her life Hell on earth. The only way it was tolerable was for my mom to create a fantasy world. Like Cinderella, my mother was second best, the put upon, less than, Other, only it was her birth mother, not the fairy tale evil stepmother who was the monster. Most of the time, my mom lived in a delusion. It was the only way she could survive. I was the product of a brief college romance, one she had hoped would be her ticket out. She held on to the idea that someday, her Prince would come and rescue her. The Princess would marry her Prince Charming and take her away from it all. Then, a new Queen would emerge.

When she'd met my stepdad, she'd found a way to escape. She only saw my grandmother a few times after that. A few hospital scares orchestrated completely on my grandmother's end and visits here and there to Rose Briar. Part of my mother's *own* fucked up allegiance, I guess. And she *never* forgave Aunt Laera for deserting her. But what she, my mother, would never realize is that the golden child and the scapegoat were both damaged. The hurtful barbs, words that cut so deep, along with the physical abuse — they were both scarred inside and out. Neither of them ever felt worthy. Neither of them ever felt like they were enough. They both walked away, beaten down, in the wake of their maniacal mother. My mom would never know that Laera had also been an injured party. I'm not giving Aunt Laera a pass…but maybe leaving was the only way she could break free.

NOW

    I was scared. Damnit, I didn't want to be, but I was. My mother slowly and quietly got up from the floor and walked over to her bed. She got back down on the floor and was reaching around under her mattress. She pulled out a DIY shank. *Oh fuck*, I thought. My mind began to race. I was looking around the room, looking for the damn buzzer to call the men in the white coats and get the hell out of here. I had to act fast. But she didn't get up. She just sat there on the floor next to her bed, playing around with her weapon.

"You know, Elia, we've always competed for center stage. It was the same with my sister Laera. Laera was the beauty. Laera was the talented one. I looked up to her. She was my champion. She did her best to keep me protected from our mother. Then she left, and I was all alone."

Competed for center stage?? With me?? I thought. Okay, she was off in la la land.

And she went on, "What is with you and the cutting, Elia? Are you so starved for attention? Even here, me, locked up in this place, unable to write, the little notice I get from the staff, did you think you'd come in here, dragging your leg, limping down the hall, and what, did you think the nurses would say, 'Oh you poor thing. Not only does a pretty young woman like you have to come in here and visit your deranged mother, but you're hurt too, you poor, poor thing.' Is that what you thought, Elia? Well, I'll tell you what, Elia, I can fix that."

This was it. I was going into panic mode. I turned as fast as I could, striking out for the door. *Got to reach the buzzer, got to get out,* was all I was thinking. My fingers were inches away from it. I glanced back quickly in case she was ready to attack, and then I realized Mother hadn't moved.

My breath caught in my throat, my lips slightly parted, and I slid down the wall and sat frozen, static. My mother was sitting on the floor next to her bed, slicing open her own ankle! I could just make out the shape of the tool she was using. It looked like two forks fused together, one end fashioned into a jagged blade. In shock, riveted to my spot, I watched as my mother carved away, blood slowly beginning to pool on the yellow linoleum floor. A few gasps escaped from her lips, but her jaw was tight. She was determined. I could not believe she wasn't making more noise. That had to hurt! She sat there a few moments more, whittling, the gash deepening, widening, muscle and sinew exposed, juicy red meat.

Then she paused. Mother flipped her handy dandy homemade shank around to the pronged end and began to dig as though, my God, my Goddess, as though she was getting ready to take a bite! She paused again, put her weapon down and brought her blood splattered hand up to cover her mouth. I hadn't moved. I was thinking, "Good,

good. She'd stopped." I was wondering what she would do next. It was at that moment she bent over, picking up her lower leg with both hands. Then, in a state of madness, she lowered her head and began to eat. *Oh my God, oh my God, oh my God*, I couldn't believe what I was seeing, but I couldn't take my eyes off of her.

She looked up at me, her eyes, my eyes, blood on her lips, a bit of her own skin dangling off her chin, hands all reddened now, and that fucked up toothy smile spread across her face, "You know what, Elia? I have longed to write since I've been cooped up in this place. I can see now my writing is not unlike your cutting. It's like an addiction, like a hunger. And now…I'm feeding myself!" She laughed, a sound coming out kind of like a "Ha ha huh," and then she got right back to it! It was like watching self-cannibalism — dinner, for one. That was it. Hysteria. She was officially over the edge. There was no coming back from this. I was able to mutter one small word, barely audible. I whispered, "Mama," as I reached for the wall behind me and placed my hand on the call button.

I was huddled in a quivering mass by the door when the orderlies came in. There were only two of them, but when they saw what was happening, they yelled for more assistance. By the time they had all come in, Mother had grabbed her shiv again and was looking at them all with her mouth full and a fork in her hand. It was chaos. Two staff came in to help me up and out. One of them put a blanket around my shoulders, and the other was asking me questions, but I didn't hear a thing. Once the door was closed, I looked back into that small, glazed window into Mother's room and watched the scene unfold before me. No more princess experiencing her happily ever after, waving as the credits ran. No, she was thrashing about, screaming now, out of her mind, a monster. The Queen was gone. It took five of them to restrain her and another one to stick her with a hypodermic in order to sedate her. The mother wound is deep. It can leave a hole, an ache that longs to be filled. I took it all in, realizing this was it. It was over. I realized my hunger had subsided, and I'd lost my appetite.

CHAPTER 14

Several weeks had passed since that day. Papers were turned in, and summer school was over. I'd upped my therapy visits to three times a week. Oh, and I'd requested regular medication, too. I mean, WTF? It would be a long damn time before I got over what went down during my last visit to The Spa, and I needed all the help I could get. After all of that, they'd moved Mother to a different floor. Visiting wasn't an option. She'd live out the rest of her days there. After what she'd done to herself, she was highly medicated daily, a life lived in a steady stupor, a haze. If you could call it a life. It was grim. Her body was now permanently mutilated; she would never be able to slide gracefully into that glass slipper.

T and I spent the remaining weeks of summer just vibing. We kept it low-key. It was all long days, strawberry sno balls, and fairy tale sunsets by the bay. Some nights, we'd spend at her house. And now that I had my house all to myself, T would come over some days, and we'd move furniture around and redecorate. We even painted my room! No more drab white. Somehow, I'd let T talk me into painting my walls purple! We'd turn the music up loud, draw on our tablets, talk about what senior year would be like, and stay up til all hours watching scary movies. T just humored me with this pastime. Me, I loved the spooky, the bizarre. In a horror movie, you could escape the everyday, let your mind go someplace else. There were times when the action was so preposterous, so out of left field, you had to laugh. Or I did, anyway. These movies made my life look normal! I didn't like the gore anymore, though. *Too* much blood and guts. Oh…I'm also a vegetarian now.

And there were times I had the house all to myself. There was no indication that any ghosts were hanging around, bad or good. One day, when I felt ready, I headed up to Mom's old attic room. I had the guts to peek into the closet where she'd shut me in that time. Huh. There was nothing there. The little furniture that had been in there was gone, and it looked like it had been cleaned. That must have been the work of my stepdad before he'd left, still trying to clean up Mom's messes. Now, it was time to explore what was behind that smaller door. I'd found a bunch of keys in the kitchen junk drawer and had tried a few until I found the right one. Opening the door, I climbed up a few stairs. It wasn't like a whole other floor or a whole other attic space, just three or four steps. Then it opened up to a room smaller than my mom's but bigger than a walk-in closet. I looked around. There wasn't much to see. Some light came in through a high window. There was a box marked BOOKS, an old trunk, and there, off to the side, was the vanity and the mirror that had been in that other closet. I wonder why my stepdad had put that in here? Why didn't he get rid of it along with Mom's other stuff?

I walked over and stood in front of the mirror. I began to think about Persephone, living in Hell with the undead. She had her ghosts, and I had mine. Or did I? It was hard to come to grips with that. I knew I'd seen them, felt them, their hold so tight on me at times. But had they really been there after all? Then I heard something. Oh, shit, what was that? I looked behind me. A fucking rat. Damnit, I'd have to do something about that. Maybe call an exterminator? My stepdad would pay for that, I was sure. Then I turned back to the mirror, and there in the reflection, standing behind me, all hunched over, pale, skin sagging, dark holes where eyes should have been, was my Aunt Laera. "Ouch! The hell Aunt Laera?" I said. She'd grazed the skin on the back of my neck with her nails, scratching me. She was only there for a second, maybe two, but I'd seen her. Then, she disappeared, leaving only the scent of vanilla in the air. I felt a little nauseous. I rubbed my neck where her nails had just made contact. Then, I looked at my hand. She hadn't drawn blood, so that was good. Deep breath. "Um...Okay," I muttered. That was enough exploration for now. Time to go back downstairs.

After *that*, I knew rest would not come easily. The therapist had given me something for that, too. I sat down on my bed, popped a couple of pills, and took a sip of water. As I lay there, looking at my purple walls, I thought about all of The Horrifying Women from my line. Most of them were gone, though I guess there must have been some reason Aunt Laera was still here. I'd have to get with Kelly about fixing that one. I don't think my stepdad would pay for me to bring in a team of paranormal investigators, though. My eyelids were getting heavier and heavier. I hated taking pills. They were like poison, but at this point, I didn't know what else to do. I needed to sleep, to escape. After all, I was one of them too — The Horrifying Women — whether I liked it or not; it was in my blood. I still had some work to do, but for now, I let myself drift off to sweet sleep.

Author's Note

I began to create *Wounded* in November of 2021. Ideas started to float around in my head, coming at me from three distinct inspirations. The first being an image from a dream that I couldn't shake. In *Wounded*, Elia's Mom is the one who is having dinner for one. In my dream, it was an injured frog. I have an irrational fear of frogs, but that's fodder for another story. Secondly, it was also around that time that I was researching the use of fairy tales in storytelling. I'd like to thank Dr. Sara Cleto and Dr. Brittany Warman for developing the course, "Spellcraft, Write like a Witch." I utilized the information in their passage on "How to Write a Fairy Tale," detailing Vladimir Prop's 31 functions as a way to loosely structure my story. Lastly, I enjoy being up in my head a lot, deciphering what I think and why I think it—there's a lot going on up there! I like to read a lot of horror myself, and I like it when an author uses horror as the framework for telling a good tale. I thought I could do it too!

You may ask why I write nonfiction and fiction and why I write about personal growth and have a love for horror. One is to help keep myself out of the mental institution. One is to offer a glimpse within. You, the reader, can decide which is which. Maybe "I'll be taken away, ha ha."

I'd like to include a note about the song "They're Coming to Take Me Away, Ha-Haaa!" This song was written and performed by Jerry Samuels (billed as Napoleon XIV) and released on Warner Bros. Records in 1966. The flip or B-side of the single was simply the A-side played in reverse, and given the title "!aaaH-aH,yawA eM ekaT oT gnimoC er'yehT" (or "Ha-Haaa! Away, Me Take to Coming They're") and the performer billed as XIV NAPOLEON. Weird, huh? Thank you, Wikipedia. "They're Coming to Take Me Away, Ha-Haaa!" climbed the charts initially, but radio stations across the country banned the record after receiving complaints from doctors and institutions claiming that the song shamed and mocked the mentally ill.

Another song or chant I'd like to pay homage to is the song that the Girls closed their ceremonies with. "May the Circle Be Open" is credited to Robert Gass and can be found on *Chanting: Discovering Spirit in Sound — The Best of Robert Gass and On Wings of Song.*

Acknowledgements

First, thank you to Karen Fuller, my editor. You helped me take my story from good to great! Thank you for your patience and hard work. Thanks to Jada Duffy, my extra pair of eyes. Jada, your feedback was tremendous, and I hope in the end, you could *see* the people, *smell* the smells, and *feel* the fright. Sorry, I gave you nightmares! The women in *Wounded* are fiction naturally, but my real life green-haired tattooed friend, Kristen, helped Kelly come to life on the page. My early readers, Keisha, Natalie, and Rachel, thanks for your time, your feedback, and your friendship— you're some of my favorite ghouls. Thanks to Ellie, my computer genius. Your help was illuminating and necessary! A special thank you to Adam Martin. Your cover art is tremendous. Can't wait to work with you again on another project. Robert P. Ottone, your blurb for Wounded is greatly appreciated. Your book, *The Vile Thing We Created*, was my favorite summer read! This is when the internet works! You can reach out and find connection and kindness. I am deeply honored and grateful for your contribution. And finally, I thank my daughters, Amelia and Meredith. You are my heart, and I'd give my blood for you. This book is for you both. Always know you can do anything you set your mind to! May you two grow up feeling loved and free.

Greta T. Bates

About the Author

Greta T. Bates lives in sunny Fairhope, AL, where she draws the drapes and writes in the dark. She published *Snapping, Fraying and Dangling in the Wind*, *Thoughts on Motherhood, Midlife and a Meaningful Existence* in 2020. Currently, she is writing short stories that explore lost love, revenge, and facing one's fears, told through the lens of horror. A Mills College alumna, Greta, has been published in Eternal Haunted Summer-Pagan Songs and Tales, Summer Solstice 2022 issue, with Scars Publications at scars.tv, Down in the Dirt Magazine, Siren's Call, Trembling With Fear, The Mythos Minute Podcast, and in Horror Scope-A Zodiac Anthology, volumes 1 and 3 edited by H.

Everend. *Wounded* is her first novella.

You can find her at https://www.gretabateswrites.wix.com/gretatbatesauthor or at www.instagram.com/greta_t_bates.

Author Photo Credit: Amanda Root

Made in the USA
Columbia, SC
13 September 2023

22822055R00109